For Kari

XOXO

D1636497

Red Havoc Rogue

(Red Havoc Panthers, Book 1)

T. S. JOYCE

Red Havoc Rogue

ISBN-13: 978-1543023848
ISBN-10: 1543023843
Copyright © 2017, T. S. Joyce
First electronic publication: February 2017

T. S. Joyce
www. tsjoyce.com

NOTE FROM THE AUTHOR:

This book is a work of fiction. The names, characters, places, and incidents are products of the writer's imagination or have been used fictitiously and are not to be construed as real. Any resemblance to persons, living or dead, actual events, locale or organizations is entirely coincidental. The author does not have any control over and does not assume any responsibility for third-party websites or their content.

Published in the United States of America

First digital publication: February 2017
First print publication: February 2017

Editing: Corinne DeMaagd
Cover Photography: Wander Aguiar
Cover Model: Jonny James

DEDICATION

For Tacos.

ACKNOWLEDGMENTS

I couldn't write these books without some amazing people behind me. A huge thanks to Corinne DeMaagd, for helping me to polish my books, and for being an amazing and supportive friend. Looking back on our journey here, it makes me smile so big. You are an incredible teammate, C! Thanks to Wander Aguiar and his amazing team for this shot of Jonny James for the cover.

And also a big thank you to Jonny James, the cover model for this book. I get the chance to meet and work with some incredible people in this industry, and he is one who surprised me in good ways.

To my cubs, who put up with so much to share me with these characters, my heart is yours. You keep thanking me for working so hard for you, but that always blows my mind. You are worth every ounce of effort, no thanks needed. You are the amazing ones.

And last but never least, thank you, awesome reader. You have done more for me and my stories than I can even explain on this teeny page. You found my books, and ran with them, and every share, review, and comment makes release days so incredibly special to me.

1010 is magic and so are you.

ONE

Annalise Sutter leaned against the open doorframe to the cage room and crossed her arms over her chest as she blew out a long sigh. This was goodbye to her old life and hello to her new one.

The walls were covered in claw marks from the animal inside her. Strips of floral wallpaper hung in tatters down the wall, the single mattress in the corner was shredded and leaking fluff and bedsprings, and there were several holes in the sheetrock that exposed the metal bars her brother, Samuel, had built into the walls to keep her from escaping and mauling the neighbors.

The panther inside of her was insane.

She was a rip-roaring, razor-clawed brawler set

on bleeding anything that dared to breathe around her. Samuel had jokingly named her "Angel" after the first time he'd met the panther. She-Devil was more like it. She-Devil ripped out of her whenever she felt like it and went insane, sometimes for days. Six months of this—fearing the monster in her middle— and Samuel had found her a shot at a new life with some panther shifter crew out in the boonies. Probably a bunch of smelly mountain men living in the trees or wherever it was that panther shifters liked to live.

Her phone dinged, and a sudden wave of butterflies fluttered around in her stomach. It was *him*. She knew it before she pulled it from her pocket and opened the home screen. As she read his name on the caller ID, a sudden wave of sadness overwhelmed her. Saying goodbye to her old life meant saying goodbye to Jaxon, and he was the only thing that had kept her steady as she'd transitioned into this person she didn't recognize.

Hey, Anna. Thinking about you and wishing you were here. The sun's setting over the falls.

Her phone dinged again, and a picture of a pretty orange sunset came through. The sun was sinking between two mountains in the distance, and in front was a gently rolling river. It was stunning, and she wished more than anything she was a normal girl who could share a sunset with a normal man like him.

She smiled sadly and typed in, *What would you do if I walked up behind you and wrapped my arms around your middle right now, and told you not to turn around, just be with me until the sun disappears between those two mountains?* Send. Yeah, she was feeling mushy. She'd been putting off her goodbye.

A response came a few seconds later. *I'd say okay, but I would put your hand down the front of my pants while we watched it.*

She giggled. He was good at surprising her out of melancholy moods. She would miss that the most. *How was work?* Send.

The front door banged open and Samuel called, "Annalise, are you ready to go? We're burnin' daylight. Is this all you packed? And why the fuck is your suitcase purple? What happened to the black ones dad got you?"

Annalise snarled up her lip at the pain of the mention of her parents. She'd had to back off the relationship with them to protect them from She-

Devil. Maybe someday, if she could get the panther under control, she could hug them again. Annalise made her way out of the cage room and into the living room. "I didn't want us to have matching luggage anymore, Samuel. I like purple." Samuel's blue eyes flashed with disgust as he hauled her luggage out the front door. Her house was small, but it was hers. Or it had been until she'd been forced to break the lease by Mr. Toots. That was what she called her landlord, even though his real name was Daniel Poots, which was almost just as bad. It was either move out or he would go to the hometown newspaper about her panther and force her to register as a shifter.

Fuck that, Mr. Toots. She-Devil was a secret Annalise would go to her grave with.

Her phone chirped. *Work was dirty. Just getting off. Cracking open a beer. What are you doing? Send me a pic.*

A naughty pic? Send.

I like where your head's at, but no. Send me a pic of what you're doing. I feel really fucking far away from you lately.

What do you mean? Send.

You know what I mean. You've been quiet. Something's going on that you aren't telling me. Pic please. Convince me you haven't moved on already.

Just to test him, she typed out, *Did you follow that story about Dark Kane?* Send.

Dark Kane?

Yeah, the dragon shifter that burned the Smoky Mountains? Send.

Samuel was waving her to the car now, looking frustrated as hell that she was taking so long. It was an all-day drive where they were going. She put one finger up and closed the door so she could do this in private. Jaxon was stalling on answering. He always did this when he didn't want to talk about something. That man was a closed-off mystery who only gave her the barest hints of his life. And she'd been totally addicted to unravelling the complicated ball of tangled yarn that he was. She'd breathed for the moments when he would slip up and tell her something real.

But this is where the distraction stopped. She had to focus now on fixing her life. Annalise's stomach hurt so bad, she wanted to double over the pain. She missed him already.

The phone chirped. *You know I don't follow that shifter shit. What's going on?*

Jaxon was anti-shifter, and she was the most volatile one. He was human, and she'd made a huge mistake that had stolen her humanity away. She was about to go live in the Appalachian Mountains, cut off from everything she knew. She would never hug him, or hold his hand, or go to the movies or grocery shopping, or sleep beside him or any of a hundred thousand things she'd imagined doing with him over the past few months.

They were both too different.

No, not just different.

They were incompatible.

I've missed you. Send.

Then stop missing me, Anna. Tell me what's going on. I can help you fix it. I'm right here.

Tears welled up in her eyes as she opened the door slowly and took a picture of her brother leaned up against the car, arms crossed, glaring at her. And then she did something that would hurt her for always because it would hurt someone she had grown to care for deeply.

She sent the picture of her brother and typed out,

The distance you felt was real. I have moved on. It's moving day. I'm moving in with him. I'm so sorry. Send.

Shoulders heaving with her emotions, she rushed to the kitchen sink and dropped her phone into a bowl of water that sat inside. If she didn't cut herself off completely, she would get weak and crawl back. She would drag both of their hearts through this because she couldn't help herself. Jaxon was her addiction. He was happy moments when she'd been struggling to find them before. Even if he was full of secrets and closed off half the time, he still felt steady.

Hands shaking, she clenched them at her sides and forced herself to leave the phone drowning in the water. It was done. No more leading him on, no more pretending she could have a normal life with someone like him.

It was high time she, Annalise Sutter, accepted that she was a shifter.

She couldn't depend on Jaxon to keep her steady now.

If she wanted any kind of stable life back, she would have to depend on the Red Havoc Crew.

TWO

"Son of a bag of dicks," Jaxon muttered as he looked over the steering wheel of his truck to what definitely resembled a moonshiner's camp. This was not at all the hotel he'd been told Annalise would be at. He'd been duped.

Jaxon rolled down the window halfway, scented the fresh Virginia forest smells, and promptly gagged. It smelled like cat piss. Mother fucker.

As seven different revenges played across his mind, he connected a call back home to Damon's Mountains.

"Hey, Jax!"

"Bash, please tell me you didn't send me straight into panther territory to find Annalise."

There were a few moments of silence before the best stalker-slash-hunter in the Boarlander crew lowered his voice. "Your mom made me not tell you. She's scary."

Jaxon scrubbed his hand over his face tiredly and then strangled the wheel with his free hand. "Is she there?"

"No?" The brawler bear shifter didn't even try to hide the lie in his voice.

"Bash!"

"She's been waiting for you to call me. We're eating Twinkies and drinking beer on my front porch. Your dad and brother are here, too."

"Hey dickweed," his twin brother, Jathan, called through the line.

"Oh God, this is my nightmare," Jaxon muttered.

"I had a nightmare last night, too," Bash said solemnly. "I dreamed that I accidentally told you that Annalise was a panther shifter, and your mom made the grocery store stop selling pizza rolls like she said she was gonna do, and I couldn't figure out how to special-order the pepperoni ones, and they would only deliver cheese ones—"

"Give me the phone," Ma muttered across the line.

There was a blast of static and then, "Hey, baby boy."

"Ma, what the fuck? She's a panther?"

"First off, don't use the word fuck with me unless you do that curse justice. Second, I had good reasons for keeping her big-catness quiet."

"Just…" Jax counted to three in his head and prayed for patience. "Please tell me what's going on."

"Okay, pinky swear me you won't get mad."

"No."

"Fine. I accidentally made Bash research her when you first started talking, and I know how you feel about dating shifters, so I accidentally kept it a secret that she wasn't human. Did you bring the green M&Ms?"

Jaxon blew out a soft, steadying breath and did another three-count before answering carefully. "Why would I bring her candy right now?"

"Orange M&M's will make her boobs grow, but I've seen a picture of your girl, and she's got plenty. You don't need those. Green M&M's will make her horny. You're welcome."

Jaxon stared defeatedly out the window, shaking his head as he watched a pair of birds on a low-hanging branch. His ma, Willamena Madden, aka

Willa Barns, aka Almost Alpha, aka Second of the Gray Back Crew was a handful on a good day. But right now, she was being ridiculous.

"Hey," Jathan crowed in the background. "Remember that one time Jaxon dated a panther shifter for four months and didn't even know it?" The slap of hands sounded, and Jaxon could just imagine him high-fiving his dad. This was the worst day ever.

A freaking panther shifter? He wanted to kick everything. He'd been epically lied to, not only by the girl he'd been talking to for months, but by his family and Bash. And now several things Annalise had said or hinted at made sense. She'd been asking him more about shifter stuff lately, like she was testing him. He'd thought she had figured out he was a grizzly shifter and had been avoiding her questions like the plague. His views on his animal were...complicated.

And now his views on Annalise were pretty damn complicated, too. If Bash was right, and she was here, she was in the heart of a notoriously private, violent, and reclusive crew of panthers. Jax's bear was a brawler, but he didn't know enough about this crew to go in there guns blazing and asking what the fuck Annalise meant by ditching him all the sudden three days ago. He knew the picture she sent was of her brother, but she'd gotten rid of her phone or something and hadn't picked up in days.

Stupid him, he'd thought she was in trouble, and he was here on some half-cocked rescue mission to get her out of whatever danger she'd found, but nope, she was just a damn big cat, doing big cat shit. Girls were complicated enough without claws.

Fuck, he'd really liked Annalise, but big cats and bears didn't mix.

"Don't run," Ma said through the phone, like she could read his mind. He hated when she guessed his feelings. "See why she moved out there at least. She hasn't been a part of a crew before now, so something happened. You owe it to yourself to at least see her tits."

"Ma," he gritted out.

"I meant see her." There was the crinkle of paper, and then she was chewing loudly in the phone.

"Ma, listen to your maternal instincts and share," Jathan demanded.

"Boy, I love you, but I'm not sharing my Twinkie with you. You're a grown man. Go get your own."

Tiredly, Jaxon muttered, "I'm hanging up now."

"Don't forget to expose your neck, boy," Dad called through the phone.

Unease unfurled deep in his gut. "What do you mean?"

"If you're in panther territory, they'll be hunting you already. Put up a fight, but if you're losing too badly, expose that neck and hope they don't go for the jugular. Good luck getting boned."

"Fight good! Bye, baby," Ma sang.

"I'm kind of sorry, Jax!" Bash rushed out right before the line went dead.

Jaxon dropped the phone in the cup holder and threw the truck into gear. Hell no to all of this. He was out of here. He needed to regroup at a local hotel and figure out his next move, but he was definitely not ready to go to war with the panthers over Annalise. If he was perfectly honest, he was pissed at her for lying.

Jaxon spun his tires out on the grass. The headlights were facing the road again before he noticed the red-headed man standing in the middle of the dirt track. His blazing gold eyes were hard as stones, his head canted, his mouth set in a grim line of fury, and every muscle in his body tense. Sheeyit.

With a snarl, Jaxon slammed on the brakes and shoved the truck into park. His bear was right there now, ready to fight, just like always when he saw another male shifter. He pushed open the door and was pulling off his shirt the second his shoes hit the soggy ground.

"Careful," the man drawled in a voice too low and gravelly to be human. "You're in my territory. You'll answer questions before we bleed. Why are you here, *Jaxon Barns*?"

Great, this man knew him, but Jaxon didn't know a damn thing about him. He hated this kind of disadvantage. "You know my name, so you know who will come raining fire if I don't make it back home."

"Damon? Damon doesn't scare me, Grizzly. I could have Dark Kane here much sooner than the blue dragon could burn my woods. Let's not put our friends at war though, yeah?"

"Are you the alpha here?"

The man dipped his chin once, and his eyes blazed even brighter. Movement caught his attention to the right, and when Jaxon glanced over, there was a tall man with a single scar down his face, arms crossed over his chest. He spat and leaned languidly against the trunk of a tree. Jaxon wasn't often snuck up on, so in a bout of self-preservation, he scanned the rest of the woods to find two more men. One was squatted down in the dirt, glaring up at him from ten yards off, and one was sitting up on a thick, low-hanging branch, one leg draped over the side, as he cut chunks of red apple with a foot-long bowie knife. That one smiled at him like a psychopath right before he popped a sliver of fruit into his maw.

Four cats, and he could take them easily. Still, he was careful where he waged war. He'd seen too much in Damon's Mountains to waltz into fights unprepared, and he didn't know much about the reclusive panther crew. They could have a dozen more hiding in the woods for all he knew. "Look, I'm not here for any trouble. This is all just a misunderstanding. I was looking for this girl—"

"What girl?" the alpha asked.

Jaxon narrowed his eyes and scrubbed his hand down his jaw. He might be pissed at Annalise for lying, but it still didn't feel right putting her name in front of these backwoods shifters if she wasn't here. The instinct to protect her was still strong as ever. "Clearly, she's not here, so it doesn't matter."

"You talkin' about the dumb one?" the man in the tree asked. "The one with no instincts at all?"

Pursing his lips, Jaxon angled his head in denial. "Nope. She's smart."

"Human smart or shifter smart?" the man squatting in the dirt asked. "We got a newcomer here who is one, but not the other."

"Anson!" the alpha snarled.

"Well what, Ben? If he wants her, he should take her straight outta here and save us all some misery. I mean"—he shrugged and gave a quick gesture to the woods—"where is she? Surely she can hear a big-ass loud truck in her territory, but she's probably holed up in her room, paintin' her nails or doin' a facial or whatever other dumb shit pretty girls like her do."

"Annalise?" Jaxon asked.

"That's the one," the man in the tree said, waving the tip of his knife toward the road. "We call her Princess Panther."

"Why are we talking and not killing?" asked the tall man leaning up against the tree.

"Barret, I've told you, we can't kill everyone who drifts through our woods," Ben murmured.

Dark eyebrows arched high, Barret asked, "Why

not? I know like six ways to hide a body."

"You know six?" Bowie Knife asked, leaping gracefully from the tree and landing with almost no impact on his legs. "Bullshit, list them."

Barret lifted his middle finger. "One, alligators."

"Oh, God, here we go," Anson said, rolling his head back.

"Two," Barret said, lifting his pointer finger, "we could call Dark Kane to eat all the bodies."

The alpha rolled his eyes and threw his head back. He inhaled deeply and released the breath in a puff. "Can we talk about this dumb shit literally any other time than right now when we're supposed to look like we aren't idiots."

"He's a bear shifter," Anson said in a thick southern accent.

"So?" Ben asked.

"So, who gives a fuck what he thinks because he's a *bear shifter*."

Bowie Knife snorted.

"Annalise isn't up for grabs, Grizzly," Ben said, running a hand over his cropped blond hair. "If I were you, I'd get out of here while the gettin' is good."

But Jaxon hesitated. She was really here. Ben and

his crew had confirmed it. She was so close he could practically feel her, smell her, and he imagined what tasting her would be like. He'd been doing this for four months, wishing he could be close enough to see her, and now he was within spitting distance. And yeah, he was angry she'd been a lying little liar. But he also wanted to see if their connection in real life could be as strong as it was through those text messages.

Fuck, he was gonna bleed today. *Fight good.* Ma's voice rang in his head as he kicked at the mud with the toe of his work boot. "I can't leave without seeing her."

"Can we kill him now?" Barret asked.

Jaxon chuckled and shook his head. "You can try, kitty cat. I don't die easy, though."

"Last chance, Grizzly, because you ain't seein' Annalise," Ben said. "She's part of my crew, and panthers don't mix with other shifters. Everybody knows that, so don't push me on this one or I'll let Barret have you."

"And me," Anson said.

"And me," Bowie Knife muttered, chucking his knife at the ground. It flung end over end and stuck blade first. And then he pulled his shirt off smoothly to reveal a chest that was scarred to hell. These boys were brawlers and dominant, every last one of them. Jaxon cursed Bash and Ma for not giving him more of a head's up. He could've come and stolen Annalise in the night, caveman style, and saved himself some scars if he'd known she was in hillbilly panther-land.

A smattering of pops sounded, and the scent of fur hit Jaxon's nose just as he looked over at Barret. He was already Changed into a massive black panther and was charging Jaxon. Shit, he was fast. The echo of bones breaking filled the clearing around the road, and then his own Change came out of nowhere since his inner grizzly was pissed.

Barret barreled into him and slammed him into the side of the truck just as his bear hit the ground on all fours.

And then there were claws, teeth, and pain.

THREE

The scream of a panther made Annalise sit up straight in bed. Frozen, she sat there, ears straining, staring at the door of her single room cabin. Perhaps she'd imagined it.

A deep, terrifying, and unfamiliar roar shook the entire house.

"Oh, my gosh," she murmured, flying into action.

Something was wrong. They were under attack, or the police were here, or they were at war with another crew, or something equally bad. She just knew it.

Instincts blaring, Annalise threw open the door and looked frantically around. Two cabins down, Jenny, the alpha's mate, stood staring at the woods, her six-year-old son, Raif, gathered against the front of her. She cast Annalise a worried glance, her shoulder-length brunette locks twitching with the movement.

"Not much scares the boys," she murmured, "but if it's a grizzly shifter...it's bad news."

"What do we do?"

Another roar sounded, followed by the screams of two panthers.

"Jenny, what do we do?" Annalise repeated louder as panic did something awful to the animal inside of her.

Jenny sighed. "We kill it."

Annalise's legs were moving before she fully registered what Jenny had uttered. Kill it? She'd seen bear shifters before on television. They were monstrous things, massive bruins twice the size of panthers. Three times, perhaps. But kill it? She didn't even know why she was running through the woods right now. She didn't understand her panther's reaction, but now she could smell fur and blood, and the fighting was so loud it made her dizzy.

A tree root came out of nowhere, tripping her, and with a cry, she pitched forward. Before she hit the ground, something more terrifying than a grizzly in her new territory happened. Her panther exploded from her.

And now she was going to kill everyone.

She wanted to sob and scream, "No!" and tuck herself back into her human skin so she wouldn't hurt anyone, but it was too late. She-Devil was out.

The Red Havoc Woods blurred by, and her stomach dipped with how fast she was in this body. She was a black-furred bullet headed straight into the heart of the fight. This was what She-Devil lived for—bleeding things. Ben and the crew were going to be so mad at her.

Through a break in the trees, she could make out the clearing around the single dirt lane that wound through the forest. Parked near the trees was a giant, jacked-up silver Dodge Ram that was a damn monster truck, and beside it was the battle she'd heard. The grizzly was bigger than any she'd seen in the news. It had reddish brown fur and black, six-inch claws that arched through the air as he swatted a panther across the ribs and sent it flying into a tree. It's glowing green eyes sparked with intense fury as he swung around to the cat currently biting the muscular hump on his back. He reached over his shoulder and ripped it off with such violence, it should've stopped her in her tracks.

Kill the cats.

What? No, you are one of the cats. Defend the cats. Protect the bear.

What the fuck was happening? She couldn't stop or slow down, and she was only yards away. And for an instant, that horrifying, terrifying monster bear locked gazes with hers, and there was a spark of something she didn't understand. She bunched her muscles, prepared to force this body to leap onto his back and rip into his exposed throat as he was busy with one of the panthers, but she put too much power into her jump and instead sailed over his back and slammed into Ben, who had been jumping for the bear at the same time. At least she thought it was Ben. It smelled like him as they hit the grown like a pair of missiles. The wind was nearly knocked from her, but that didn't stop She-Devil, no. She went to war with her damn alpha, and he went to war right back.

Pain slashed against her shoulder as she sank her teeth into his neck. God, he was strong, and so fast he blurred. A good fighter, but he lacked the insane fury that She-Devil was fueled by. Claws raked down her back, and she was pulled hard. The other panthers were there, trying to separate her from their alpha.

Fuckers. Pulling her off a kill like this? They were gonna die too then. Annalise spun and slashed her claws across the face of a green-eyed panther— Barret probably.

The bear stood behind Barret and roared a long, deafening sound. It felt like he was calling to her. That wasn't right...was it? She wanted to run to him. She wanted to place herself between him and the crew and dare these assholes to fight her. Nobody was killing the grizzly today. Not today...not ever. Ever? God, what was wrong with her?

Ben was going to kick her out of the crew for how damaged she was. This was the part she had been trying to hide for the last three days. Completely out of control of her body, Annalise swung to the side, bolted around a very surprised looking Barret, and charged the bear. He didn't even move, didn't back up a single step, just locked eyes on Annalise and watched her skid to a stop in front of him.

And then she did something unforgiveable.

She turned on her crew.

Yep, she, the biggest dumbass in the history of shifters, gave a murderous grizzly bear in the heat of battle her exposed back while she turned on the only people who would protect her.

She-Devil was clearly suicidal.

The crew didn't attack. Two of them slunk back and forth in tight paces, and two of them, Ben included, looked like they would probably eat her if they were dragon shifters.

Ben approached slowly, his massive paws making prints the size of dinner plates in the mud. Annalise hissed. Close enough.

Ben's gold eyes with the tiny pupils narrowed dangerously on her. He hunched into himself, and the alpha of the Red Havoc Crew Changed back into his human form. What was he doing? The grizzly could kill him so easily. But when she looked over her shoulder, the bear had backed himself across the road and was pacing the tree line, eyes on her. He shook his head as though dizzy, or perhaps confused. *Welcome to the club, Griz.* She confused the hell out of herself, too.

"Change back," Ben demanded. Power pulsed

through those two words and brushed against her skin, making her want to do…something.

The other panthers had an immediate response to Ben's order, and their bodies broke in a painful-looking way. Anson pitched forward on his hands and knees and muttered, "Fuck, Ben. You could've just asked," as pain washed across his features.

"I said Change back!" he yelled at Annalise.

She hunched down, but She-Devil liked this body and didn't give it up easy. Sorry Ben.

The sound of something big approaching too fast from behind startled her, and she turned to see the bear charging the alpha. Oh, shit. It was a bluff, thank God, and he skidded to a stop right behind her. Grunting on every exhale, eyes full of fire and locked on Ben, the grizzly was promising a quick death. Tension roiled from him, and for the first time, Annalise was actually scared. He was a monster, and on closer inspection, she could see the mash-up of claw marks on his body and older scars that had kept his fur from growing back in places.

The click of metal on metal was deafening in that silent moment. In the woods stood Jenny, huge long-range rifle aimed right for the middle of the bear's forehead. "Get the fuck out of here if you want to keep your brains from painting my goddamn woods."

The moment was so charged, Annalise's body seized with the tension, and in an instant, She-Devil was giving Annalise her body back. Her Change was painful, but fast. Annalise sat with her knees tucked under her, gasping for air as she waited for her body to make sense again. She hated the gun pointed at the bear, but for the life of her, she couldn't figure out why. He was a stranger and had brought violence to the crew. And if she was honest, she was pissed he'd made her betray Red Havoc. This was her shot at gaining a normal-ish life someday, and he'd just ruined it for her.

"Please leave," she ground out.

The grizzly turned his massive block head toward her, gave her a hard, calculating look, and then strode toward the truck. His Change was fluid, like magic. He was bear, and then he was a man. A muscular man with wide shoulders, who stood over six-foot-tall and had tattoos down his neck and back. The claw marks on his body streamed red, but he didn't limp or favor his injuries. His bare ass was perfection over long, strong legs moving in a smooth, effortless gait. He had black hair that was longer up top, but shaved short on the sides, and his giant fists were balled with anger. God, she wished he would turn and show his face so she could see if it was as beautiful as the rest of him.

He slid into the driver's side and slammed the door so hard the truck rocked with the force. The engine roared to life, and as he pulled slowly onto the road, Annalise covered her boobs with her hands in a last-minute fit of modesty.

There are some moments in life that draw you up, and etch themselves so eternally and so fully on your brain, that flashbacks will happen for years to come. Maybe forever. Annalise had one of those moments now as watched the stoic profile of the bear shifter she'd just protected.

He had a trimmed, black beard and a striking, masculine profile. His tattoos were stark against the pale skin of his neck, and right as the truck passed, he turned and locked eyes with her.

Annalise gasped in shock. It was the man who had kept her steady for the last four months. Jax had sent her a picture once. It had been blurry, just of his face, and his dark hair had been longer and shaggy, falling in front of eyes. It was a picture he'd taken before he got the ink on his neck, but she would recognize those light brown eyes and their shape anywhere. She had obsessed with that picture in her hardest moments, had memorized every facet of his face.

"Jaxon?" she murmured softly.

He looked different from the picture in subtle ways. Hardened and harsh, like a warrior instead of the sweet man she'd been talking to.

He ripped his gaze away from her and hit the gas, filling the woods with the sound of his roaring engine. Mud sprayed out from the sides of his tires as he disappeared down the road.

She'd just had a moment with the man of her dreams...but Jaxon was nothing like what he'd portrayed himself to be.

And clearly, he'd just learned, that neither was she.

FOUR

She couldn't get Jaxon off her mind. Which was bad, because right now, she was supposed to be paying attention.

"And furthermore, way to be the worst crew member in the goddamn world, Princess!" Barret yelled. "You know you're supposed to fight *with* us, right?" He pointed to the long, half-healed claw marks down his face with a shaking pointer finger. "Not against us!"

Jenny swatted his hand out of the way and slathered on another layer of scar cream. Barret snarled at her, but Jenny growled right back and didn't back down an inch.

"How do you know Jaxon?" Ben asked from

where he sat at his four-seater table with his boot propped up on an empty chair and his arms across his chest. His eyes still weren't his normal human blue. They blazed gold like the sun.

"What had happened was...I met him on this dating site, and we were just talking as friends—"

"How many dirty pictures did you send your friend," Anson asked.

"Rude, and none of your business."

Anson barked out, "I'm asking with a purpose, and you just told me more than one, so don't give us that bullshit about you're just friends. You turned on your crew!"

"You aren't my crew yet!" she fired back, good and pissed. "I haven't pledged to anyone."

"And you never will if you bring a bear around here," Ben snarled, leaning forward and resting his elbows on his knees. "Panthers. Don't. Mix. We never have. It's the rules."

"But bears and ravens and boars and gorillas and snowy owls and dragons all mix," she pointed out for the sake of arguing. All these boys were dumb as fence posts and had been mean to her for days, and she was good and done with their stupid arguments and shenanigans.

It was Jenny who spoke up, though. "How long have you been a shifter, Annalise?"

That drew her up straight on the loveseat she was currently sitting on by herself. "Not long. Six months."

"What?" asked the quietest member of the crew, Greyson. He was a big blond behemoth who she usually forgot was there until he on occasion uttered a few words. "Only six months? You were bitten?" Anger flashed through his blue eyes. "By who?"

"I'm not ready to talk about it."

"Mother fuckin' fucker," Barret drawled. "Ben seriously? We're bringing a brand new bitten she-panther into the crew? This is the worst idea. Sniff her! She's near her heat cycle, and she's already bringing in the damn bears from Damon's Mountains. Kick her out before she gets us all killed."

"It's not that simple," Ben murmured, staring at his hands as he rubbed them together. She hadn't ever seen him duck his gaze in the three days she'd been here.

"It is that simple," Barret snarled. "Kick her out and choose your crew! She clawed me protecting an enemy. Fuckin' traitor already. Look at my face, Ben.

This wasn't just some brawl for fun like the boys and I get into. This was an act of treason against her own crew."

"She doesn't have loyalty to us yet," Ben argued.

Barret winced away from Jenny's touch on his cheek and strode for the door, yanked it open, but then hesitated. "Get your head off this stupid idea, *Alpha*. She's a danger, and you have a son to protect. You have all of us to protect, and you're bringing a damn grenade into our territory and playing with the fucking pin. Three days in, and we have a grizzly fight with a Barns. With a Barns! You know who his momma is? Who his daddy is? Who his fucking brother is? He's a Gray Back, Ben. He's a *Gray Back*, and she's not important enough to die over," he said, jamming a finger at Annalise. "It's her or me, and I'm giving you time to decide. You know where I'll be until you kick her out." Barret arched his eyebrow at Ben. "Do it fast." And then he walked out the door and slammed it behind him hard enough to rattle the small cabin.

"I'm really sorry," Annalise said in desperation. "I didn't know he was a shifter! And I cut off from him and everyone else in my old life when I came here. I don't even know how he found me!"

"He has some of the best trackers in the world in his crew," Greyson said softly. "You got yourself hunted, and you put us in the middle." He sighed and pushed off the wall he'd been leaning against, then leveled Ben with a look. "I'm with Barret. She has to go. These mountains are a panther safe haven, and she's too big a risk to what we've built here." Greyson followed Barret's lead and left. At least he didn't slam the door, so there was that.

Anson followed without a word, just a narrow-eyed glare for Annalise. And then it was just her and Jenny and Ben, drowning in silence.

Annalise cleared her throat delicately. "I'm really sorry I fought you. I don't have good control over my animal—"

"Annalise, stop," Ben demanded. "You apologize too damn much. I can tell you say sorry when you're trying to keep from getting hurt, but you're a fuckin' panther now. Don't mess up. Don't make it to where we have to hear your apologies."

"Ben," Jenny said low.

"I don't know what I'm gonna do with you," he said, his blond brows arched up high. "You were already on a trial period, and you went after me and my crew on day three, woman. Day three! And the boys aren't wrong. You brought a damn Barns grizzly up here after you."

"I don't understand what his last name or family have to do with any of this," she huffed in frustration.

"You wouldn't because you don't know enough about your kind! You got bit. That sucks. It's a shitty way to become a shifter. But you should've started researching immediately. You weren't careful, you made some kind of bond with the exact type of shifter we try to keep out of these mountains, and you attracted him here. I'm gonna think on this. I have to take my crew's wants into consideration, Annalise. Until I make a decision, I forbid you to see Jaxon Barns." Ben's eyes flashed with anger before he repeated, "I *forbid* it."

Fury blasted through every cell in her body, burning her up instantly. Annalise stood in a rush and strode for the door before she gave into the urge to cuss him out. She was grown and had parents, so she sure as hell didn't need some asshole alpha making rules like he was her damn father, instead of a man she barely knew, who was the same age as her.

He was being unreasonable and prejudiced, and it wasn't fair, because yeah, she'd been thinking about Jaxon since the second she recognized the man in the truck. Not just thinking about him either, but thinking of how she could see him. There was a history and a connection there she couldn't explain to these jerk-offs who wouldn't listen to her anyway. Who would just make fun of her and tell her to turn her heart off like it was a light switch. She didn't work like that. She'd tried and failed.

Three days since she'd texted with Jaxon, and she felt like her guts had been ripped out. Loneliness had been her only companion, and she wanted that high that Jaxon had given her for all those months. The one that staved off all those thoughts of what she'd lost—her relationship with her parents, and all of her friends. Hell, she couldn't even eat in public and talk to strangers, because her eyes glowed, and she snarled uncontrollably, and Changed on a dime. She'd been cut off from everyone but Samuel, and he had his own busy life. Jaxon had been the only constant while she'd spiraled down into this awful, unfulfilling, solitary existence.

And now she had three billion questions for the

man who had been hiding the same exact monstrous secret that she had, but she was forbidden to see him? From the man who had taken the sting, and the edge from her soul-deep loneliness?

It felt like she was losing everything all over again.

Burning tears welling up in her eyes, she jogged down the stairs and bolted for her cabin. She just wanted to be inside where nobody could see the breakdown that was coming. Anson and Greyson were talking quietly near Ben's truck, and their eyes tracked her as she fled. Annalise ripped her gaze away from them and ran up the three porch stairs that led to her cabin. She was the first on the row. The door made a deafening sound as she slammed it behind her, and inside, she left the lights off so she could fall apart in the dark. It was evening, and only gray light filtered through the bay window near the small kitchen.

With a sob, she rested her forehead against the door and regretted throwing her phone in the water at her old home. She'd been so stupid. How could she have forgotten that re-reading their old messages had been medicine for her soul? When she was having a bad day, she'd watched the videos he'd made of him driving through a small town or through the woods while he talked to her. She missed the timbre of his voice and his country accent. She missed how confident he was in each syllable, missed imagining the man behind the camera as hers. She missed reading all of their silly conversations, but most of all, she missed the occasional ones that had been real. The ones where he had exposed something important about himself that made her fall a little harder for him.

But Jaxon was a ghost. He hadn't been real until today. He'd been this elusive high she could get when she looked at her phone, but today, he had become a flesh and blood man. And now she wanted to see if his arms would feel as strong around her as she'd always imagined. She wanted desperately to see if he could make her feel as safe as she'd assumed.

I forbid it.

Annalise pushed off the door and wiped her eyes furiously with the sleeve of her sweater. Ben had forbidden her to see Jaxon. He hadn't forbidden her to talk to him.

Annalise still hadn't had a chance to replace her

cell phone, but there was a landline in the kitchen. She locked the door and made her way to it, then hopped up on the counter. Feeling utterly reckless, she dialed the number she'd memorized by heart.

This was against their rules. They'd never talked on the phone, only texted. Twice she'd accidentally called him, and he'd rejected the call both times. *Please let the third time be the charm.*

It rang. And rang. And rang. When the voicemail came on—some generic woman's robotic voice telling her to leave a message—she slammed her back against the wall and dialed again.

They owed each other answers, dammit.

"Hello," came the angry, growly voice at the other end.

"Please tell me it's you," she whispered in a rush.

The line went silent. So silent that she checked she hadn't accidentally hit the button and hung up on him. "Please," she repeated.

After what felt like years, he murmured, "It's me."

"Why didn't you tell me, Jax? Why didn't you tell me you were a shifter?"

"Why didn't you tell me?"

"I asked first."

"I don't know!" There was a loaded pause and then, "Are you crying?"

She kept it quiet, but her shoulders were shaking and tears streamed down her damp cheeks. Annalise rolled her head back against the wall and stared at the exposed rafters of her cabin. When she could get words past her tightened throat, she squeaked out, "It's just really fucking good to hear your voice."

"Baaaabe," he murmured. "Fuck. Where are you? I can come back."

"No, you can't. I'm forbidden to see you."

"But you can talk to me?"

"No. I don't know. I didn't ask, I just called. I had to. Jaxon, you looked sooo…"

"So what?"

She swallowed hard as she remembered his dark hair and eyes, his height, his tattoos. "You look even better in person than in the picture you sent me."

He heaved a sigh. "Dammit, Anna, I'm so mad at you right now. I'm just pissed. You pretended you were moving in with another man. And you're a freakin' panther. If you were any other shifter…any other one…"

"What? Finish it. If I were any other shifter,

what?"

"This would be do-able. God, I don't date shifters. I never have. I want a human mate. But you sunk your damn claws in me before I knew what you were, and now my head's all messed up." His voice was so gravelly. No wonder he hadn't wanted to talk to her on the phone. She would've figured out he was a shifter just from talking to him. "Panthers don't go outside of their species to date, Anna. You live by a whole different set of rules than the rest of us. We were dead in the water from your first shift. Do you understand?"

"No," she whispered. "I don't understand any of this, Jaxon. I've only been this...this...*monster* for six months."

"What?"

"I got bit."

"Fuck, Anna!" Static blasted across the phone, causing her to wince away from the painful sound. "I need a minute," he said.

The line went dead.

She had never heard such fury in a man's voice before, and it left her shaky, and gripping the phone harder, like it was a lifeline. It felt so damn good to hear someone be angry on her behalf for what happened to her. She'd been alone with her fury for so long. Slowly, she settled it back into its cradle and slid off the counter. The conversation had ended so abruptly she didn't know what to do with herself. Was she supposed to call him back in a minute? Did he mean a literal minute?

When Samuel got worked up like this, she'd learned to give him as much time as he needed, so after a minute passed, then five and then ten, she decided to keep herself busy and give Jax a big chunk of time to work through whatever had pissed him off.

Bear shifters had bad tempers.

Well, so did panther shifters. Were all shifters just angry beings in general? Thanks to She-Devil, all signs pointed to, *hell yes*.

Absently, Annalise wiped down the already shining two-seater table with a damp rag. She'd cleaned this place from top to bottom over the last few days, just avoiding the hell out of the crew, who, if she was perfectly honest, intimidated and scared her. They were all this tight-knit group of foul-mouthed, burly, growly, giant mountain men. The alpha's mate, Jenny, would be nice to get to know, but she'd stayed closed off and spent the days in town with her son, Raif. The boys had mentioned another female in the crew, but they made the she-panther named Lynn sound like she was crazy. Not just typical emotional-woman-on-her-period kind of crazy, but certifiable. Annalise didn't even want to meet her if her animal was even more psychotic than She-Devil.

She'd wanted to tell Jaxon what had happened over the last three days so she wouldn't feel alone with this insane living situation she'd found herself in. This wasn't supposed to be her life. She'd done well in school, been raised in a perfectly normal two-parent household with her brother, gone to college, had normal boyfriends, normal friends, got a normal job at a post office in her hometown right after graduation. Her life had been set on a path of utter brown-colored normalcy since the day of her birth. Until the bite.

That one second had annihilated her entire future.

That one second that plunged her into infinite loneliness.

One second, and she was ruined.

One second, and all she could hope for with a man was what she'd built over text with Jaxon—a shallow relationship that would never go as far as touch.

She was monster now. How could she expect any man to love her the way she'd turned out to be?

The phone rang, and she jumped nearly out of her skin. Before she could stop herself, she peeled back her lips and hissed out a feral sound. God, she was weird now.

"Jaxon?" she answered.

"Come outside."

"What?"

"Come outside. Walk around your cabin and head straight back to the tree line. There is an old, wooden broken down fence about thirty yards in. It's rotted and falling down, so you'll have to look for it. There's an opening in a broken section, and behind it there is a deer trail that leads straight up the mountain. Follow it until you get out of Red Havoc territory."

"I can't just run away."

"I'm not askin' you to. You'll go back to your den tonight, cover your ass, tell your crew whatever you want. This is me giving you a choice, Anna. I'll be there on the edge of the territory. Face me. Tell me all the whys. Tell me what's happened and if you're in trouble because I can't get my animal to leave this town until I hear you say the words."

"What words?"

"That you're okay. That you don't need my help. That you don't need me. Tell me to my face, and I'll leave."

"And what if I get there and I don't want you to leave?"

Silence dragged on for eternal seconds. "Then you should tell me that to my face, too. I'll be here. Come or not, it's up to you."

"Wait. Jaxon, I have to think about this. Ben forbade me from seeing you. This crew is my shot at some kind of life where I'm not in a fucking cage. I can't just run up the mountain and disobey him. I'm already on thin ice here."

"Then no pressure, Anna. I'm not here to ruin your life. That was never what I wanted. I wanted..."

"What, Jax? Finish."

"I'll be on the edge of the territory for three hours. Bye, Anna."

Click.

Annalise strangled the phone and made a

screeching sound that hurt her throat. Ridiculous man, she couldn't just disobey Ben! She didn't know much about shifter culture, but being alpha meant he was basically mayor of Moonshine Town and she was nothing but a peon. She made to slam the phone down in the cradle, but thought better of destroying her only means of communication with the outside world and slowed it down right before it hit. Gently, and like less of a psychopath, she settled it into place.

Three hours. She glared at the bay window. It was full dark outside now, but how was she supposed to sneak by a crew of freaking panthers who heard and saw everything? She couldn't even go to the stupid communal bathroom without being watched.

She wanted to see him. There it was. She was really tempted to do this, and damn the consequences because it was Jaxon. Her entire body had gone fuzzy in the moment they'd locked eyes. He was important to her, and she couldn't even think of him driving away without seeing him first.

Maybe if she just went and told him the words he needed to hear, that would be a good compromise. Sure, she was disobeying Ben, but for a good cause...right? She was getting Jaxon the-mother-freakin'-grizzly-shifter Barns out of the territory. She was basically making up for turning on her crew in the fight. Really, she was saving them all by making him go. Or something.

But before she went, maybe she should put on some make-up and straighten her hair while she mulled over what she would say to Sexy Giant Jaxon…if she actually found the courage to do this. And maybe she should brush her teeth and smear on a second helping of deodorant to mask the scent of fur. And maybe put on cuter panties, too. Just in case.

Hmm, maybe she should call Samuel and ask him what she should do. No. This was her life now, her decision. Plus, she knew what Samuel would say, and she wanted to look at Jaxon's McHotboy face. Beard. He had a great beard. It was one of those four-day, perfectly trimmed, beautiful-man beards that made her think pervy thoughts about what kind of scratchy sensation it would cause against her sensitive inner thighs. Since he was a grizzly shifter, he would probably be bitey in the bedroom. *Oh my gosh, stop thinking about this.*

That was it. There would be no changing into cuter panties because she needed the giant granny panties to keep her pants on. Because there was no way in hell she was going to expose her purple polka-dotted comfies to any man as sexy as Jaxon Barns. These comfy cottons were her chastity belt. They would keep her on track to say what she needed to say and keep his beautiful-man beard from tickling her inner thighs.

Feeling like goddamn Wonder Woman, she slathered on powder fresh deodorant like a boss, plumped her lips with colorless Chap Stick, and pulled her thick brunette hair back in a let's-get-shit-done bun. She looked like a proud mess. Jaxon definitely wouldn't get handsy with her like this.

And if anyone stopped her, she could just say, "Look, asshole, I'm going to save all our lives, so outta my way. I have hero shit to do."

Emboldened with her terrible plan, she marched out of the cabin, looked around the empty clearing, waited a couple seconds to get caught, shrugged, and made her way to the tree line. At least She-Devil improved her night vision significantly. It wasn't even that hard to find the rotted wooden fence in the dark, or the hole with the deer trail. Up, up she climbed the path until she couldn't see the lights from the cabins behind her. Brush tripped her up time and time again, but she was determined, and the scratches on her bare legs where her shorts didn't cover would heal soon. Another advantage to She-Devil. She might want to kill every living thing around her like a little hairy serial killer, but she healed fast.

Annalise smelled Jaxon way before she saw him. He was all dominance and fur and some sexpot cologne that probably got him into a lot of girls' undies. The thought of him with other girls caused her to rattle off a snarl. When She-Devil made her imagine a pile of bodies, it reminded her of why she couldn't have pretty things—like Jaxon.

His monster truck was parked at the top of the hill, and he was leaning against it, looking down at the ground, wearing a black T-shirt and dark jeans over scuffed work boots. His arms flexed where he had them crossed over his chest, and the inky tattoos along his forearms were dark against his pale skin. His hair was messier on top than it had been earlier, as if he'd been running his hands through it. A nervous habit maybe, but it made his hair look sexy in that just-woke-up way, the kind that said he didn't care overly much about the way he looked or about being perfect.

When he noticed her, she expected his dark eyes to match the night around them, but she was surprised to find them lightened to a bright green. "You came," he said low, pushing off his truck. Jaxon lifted his chin higher and let his fists fall to his sides. Tension rolled off him in waves, and Annalise stopped in her tracks as her inner animal growled out a warning.

"I won't hurt you," he said in that deep, gravelly, inhuman voice.

"Then why do you look and feel so different?"

"Because you said you got bit." When a rumbling sound came from his chest, Jaxon shook his head hard. The sound stopped suddenly, but his eyes blazed an even brighter shade of green. It was like rain-bloated moss in the early morning. "I'm mad because someone hurt you. Who?"

Her mind skittered away from the night she became She-Devil, though. It was too hard to think about, too hard to dwell on. She'd worked very hard to block those memories completely, and he was scratching at the edge of them. She-Devil snarled and writhed inside of her.

Annalise bit her lip hard, fighting the Change her panther demanded. She dipped her gaze to his work boots. "There were times I wanted to tell you everything, but you seemed so anti-shifter, and I got scared. I didn't tell anyone this happened to me. I know you're mad, but I want you to know it wasn't just you I hid from. I cut myself off from everyone in my old life."

Jaxon ran his hand down his beard and took a careful step closer. "I wanted to tell you what I was, too."

This was the game then—trust. He had just rewarded her honesty, and now she would reward him...by taking a step toward him. He kept his eyes trained on her sneakers as she did.

"I got on that dating site because I was so lonely I thought I would die of it," she whispered, unable to hold his gaze.

Jaxon took another small step forward, and now only five yards separated them. He smelled so good.

He scratched the back of his neck and admitted, "I got on that dating site looking for a human companion."

"Why?"

"You ain't ready to talk about your bite, and I'll never be ready to talk about *why*."

"No step forward for that one, mister. You didn't give me anything."

"I'm a rogue," he ground out.

"What does that mean?"

"It means I have no crew. I never pledged to one."

"Ben said you're a Gray Back."

He made a single ticking sound behind his teeth and stared off into the woods. "Ben doesn't know me. Nobody does. That was the crew I was born into. The alpha's name is Creed. He's good. There are beasts in that crew. Brawlers and trackers. A seer. I never pledged to it though. I'm a nomad. I wander, and then I go home, and a couple days later, I wander again. Nothing holds me. Nothing anchors me."

"Did you get on that site to find an anchor?"

He dipped his chin once, blazing green eyes locked on hers.

Sadness washed through her. "And you found me instead."

Another nod.

He'd earned the three steps she took toward him.

"Admission, I came up here determined to tell

you to leave," she whispered.

He took a step. "Admission, when I drove away today, I was determined not to come back."

Step. "Admission, I'm really glad you did come back."

Step. "Admission, I want to kill whoever bit you, and I wanna do it slowly, inflicting maximum pain."

Annalise closed her eyes and inhaled sharply at how good it felt that he was protective of her. If he saw what she was really capable of, he would run, but if his animal urges matched hers, perhaps she could keep him longer. They were so close now, just a couple feet away from each other. He was tall and strong, straight-backed. Fists still clenched at his sides, chin held high and proud, eyes blazing that striking green.

"Admission." She closed her eyes tightly because she was too big a coward to watch his face when she said this part. "I always imagined what it would be like if we met, and I got to touch you. You said you wished you could hug me. That you would make a bad day okay." She dragged in a sharp, emotional breath and tried to control her emotions. "Jax, it's been a really bad fucking day. A lot of bad days actually."

The softest brush of his fingers touched her cheek, and her response was instant. She sagged forward and slid her arms up his strong chest around the back of his neck. Jaxon didn't hesitate. He bent down and lifted her against him until she had her legs wrapped around his hips. She held him tight, and his arms went strong around her back as he crushed her in place against his chest. He didn't rock them side to side, or gentle the hug. This embrace felt like desperation. He slid his massive hand up her spine to the back of her neck, and he squeezed. She should've felt trapped here against the brick wall of his solid body, held in place by his impossibly strong arms. But all she felt was safe.

"I can't have you," he whispered, his voice shaking, his arms shaking, his body shaking. "I can't fucking have you, Anna."

"Shhh," she said, burying her face against his neck. He smelled so good, familiar already somehow. His cologne, and the scent of dominance and fur. No pain, though. He didn't smell like his injuries from the fight were still hurting him. Good.

Mindlessly, she licked his throat with the very tip

of her tongue just to taste him. He gripped her hair in an instant and leaned into her, rested his whiskered cheek against hers. They were moving, but she didn't want to open her eyes to see where. She just wanted to be lost in this feeling right now. How many hundreds of times had she imagined the moment they met? How many hundreds of times had she imagined how it would feel to be wrapped around his body like this, lost in each other's embrace?

Her butt hit something cold, and she realized he'd settled her against the hood of his truck. Jaxon hadn't loosened his grip at all though, not even a little.

"Babe, I've wanted this so bad," she whispered, out of her mind with how good his strong hands felt gripping her hair and her back.

"Fuck," he said, his voice tinged with desperation. "I have to..." He eased off her and locked his muscular arms onto the cold metal of the truck, and he rested his head against her shoulder and then shook it slowly. "Anna," he murmured.

She didn't know why, but she wanted to cry. No moment had ever felt this important. Jaxon was falling apart with her. She was filled with such relief at finally, finally getting to touch him, but she also knew this was temporary. And how could they go back to not seeing each other after soul-changing moments like these?

She ran her hands through his longer hair on top and scratched them gently down his burred hair in the back just to feel the texture, just to feel him. He shivered curiously as he left his head resting against her shoulder. Slowly, he wrapped his arms around her back and stood. His bright green eyes were full of a deep emotion she didn't understand. He tilted his chin up high again, proud man, and looked like the fierce warrior she'd seen in the woods today.

"Tell me what to do."

Annalise licked her lips. "What do you want to do?"

"Real story?" That was what he'd always asked if she got onto him for joking his way through an important conversation.

She dipped her chin. "I think we should only do real stories from here on."

His blazing eyes practically glowed in the dim light as they dropped to her lips. "I wanna kiss you."

Her smile was instant, and her cheeks heated with pleasure. Her stomach filled with a fluttering sensation that she'd only ever gotten with him when he texted sweet things to her out of the blue. "You gave me butterflies again," she whispered, cupping his cheeks just to touch him. Just to feel his rough whiskers against her smooth palms. Just to be connected to him.

He turned and bit one palm gently and then straightened and slid his hands up her bare legs to her shorts, and then he gripped her hips. He was a massive man, a giant, and his hands nearly encircled her waist, but it wasn't intimidating. It was sexy as hell being so small next to him. It was nice thinking She-Devil didn't even stand a chance against his grizzly. It was nice knowing she wasn't the biggest beast here in these woods. And Jaxon was steady. He'd controlled his animal today. He'd stopped mid-charge on Ben.

Can you teach me how to be this thing? She wanted to ask him so badly, but there was some barrier between the panthers and the outside world that she didn't understand yet, so the question stayed lodged in her throat.

Jaxon's dark brows lowered slightly as he eased forward, and his hand went from her hip to trail up her ribs and then arm. Across her cheekbone, he brushed the barest touch. The corner of his lips lifted slightly.

This was happening, the moment she'd yearned for all these months. As he leaned into her, she closed her eyes and angled her face, and his lips pressed to hers. This was a first-love kiss. This was the big one a girl thought about her whole life.

Jaxon pulled her closer and inhaled deeply as he pressed his kiss more firmly onto her lips. He took her wrists in his big hands and pushed his thumbs onto her tripping pulse for just a few seconds before he smiled against her mouth and pulled her hands behind his neck. Oh God, he was good. Jaxon was like a damn professional kisser, and she was clumsy compared to him. Smooth operator. He sucked gently on her top lip and pulled her waist until their hips connected. And there was nothing sexier than this, right here, kissing on the hood of his truck, tasting each other, alone in the woods, under the full moon. Happy. Lost in each other's arms. She wanted to stay like this forever. Well...maybe not just like this. Sweet kisses were amazing with him, but her naughty hands tingled to feel his body. She controlled herself for a while, up until the point where he let off a sexy little snarl and nipped her bottom lip. Annalise let off a helpless sound and pushed her knees open wider, so his hips could rest right between her thighs, pressed up against her. Jaxon pushed his tongue past her lips and dipped it against hers, shallowly at first, but then harder and deeper and more desperate with every stroke after that. The man worked her into an inferno. Her insides turned to lava, sparking every time he gently rolled his hips. Fuck, she had to feel him.

She-Devil was making noise now, growling low and deep in her throat. Mortified, Annalise drew back and pressed her fingers against her lips, swallowed hard to try and stop the noise.

"Don't," Jaxon snarled, yanking her hand from her face as he offered her a feral smile. "I like that sound."

Annalise's eyes were probably as big as flying saucers and bright gold like the sun as she sat frozen, staring at his sexy face. Jaxon pulled her hand to his chest, which was heaving with deep breaths. His lips crashed against hers, and the gentleness was gone. Oh, he'd set them both on fire now. His rigid muscles were firm and strong under her fingertips, and just to test what he would let her get away with, she slid her flattened palm down the curve of his chest to the defined mounds of his abs. And fuck yeah, she did some math and counted those sexy things. Eight. A freaking eight-pack, and now she *needed* to feel his skin.

When she slipped her touch under the hem of his shirt and brushed her fingertips along the line of his belt, Jaxon's stomach twitched. He inhaled sharply, rested his forehead against hers for a second, and swayed toward her. And then his hand was on her neck again, pulling her in as he kissed her senseless, mindless, brainless. Instinct took over, and apparently that instinct was to meld her body to his because now she was pressed against him so tightly, there was no end and no beginning to either of them. God she loved this. Loved being locked up with him. Loved the loss of her mind, her stress, her tension. He'd always had this ability to give her an escape, and this was the best she'd ever experienced. She wasn't She-Devil anymore. Sure, the snarl was still in her throat, but there was no shame, no worry. She couldn't hurt a man like Jaxon. He was made to withstand storms and teeth and claws. He was strong enough to withstand all her ugly pieces, and somehow, someway, he was making her feel beautiful.

Feeling brave, she slid her hands up his bare stomach, then ran her nails lightly up his chest. Jaxon yanked back by inches and pulled his shirt off in one smooth motion, then guided her hands back to his skin as he kissed her again. She smiled against his lips. His desperation for her touch matched her need for his. Tomorrow would be full of regrets, but she didn't care about that right now. She just wanted to be lost in Jaxon, her great escape. She wanted to feel normal for a little while, like she wasn't a monster.

Jaxon pulled her shirt over her head and let it slip to the ground. He sucked hard on her bottom lip and then held it between his teeth as he popped the button of her jeans and ripped the zipper down. The butterflies in her stomach were rioting as he slid his hand down the front of her…granny panties. Shit.

He ended the kiss with a soft smack and glanced down. "What the hell are you wearing?" he asked through an amused grin.

Annalise clamped her arms over her lap and tensed her legs. "I hadn't intended on fooling around."

"Are these even the right size?" he asked, chuckling as he pushed her arms away and pulled at the loose hem of her ugly purple polka-dotted comfies.

"Stop," she complained, swatting at him.

"Woman, I thought I knew your underwear drawer. What about the dozen cute panty pictures you sent me? These never made the cut?"

His dark eyebrow was arched up, and he was smiling big. She was equal parts horrified and trying not to laugh to encourage him. "Go back to passionate kisses and ignore these. I don't want to laugh right now, Jaxon! I want to be turned on. And I want to turn you on. Just pretend I'm in something sexier."

He laughed harder and pulled her hand to his erection. Yep, still hard as a rock. "Anna, I don't give a shit about your panties. They're just an obstacle. I'm keeping these, though. I'm gonna frame the fucking huge things—ow!" he said, dislodging himself from where she had clamped her teeth down on his shoulder.

"You're drying me up right now, Jaxon," she muttered, crossing her arms over her chest.

"That's a lie," he rumbled, easing between her legs again and sliding his hand down the front of her panties. He buried his face against her neck and plucked at the sensitive skin there gently with his lips as he cupped her sex and slid his finger inside of her.

She gasped and gripped the back of his head as she rocked against his hand. He'd listened when she'd told him her neck was one of her favorite places for a man to pay attention to, but paired with him pushing into her just about did her in.

He sucked hard on her neck, hard enough to bruise, but she liked it. She hoped it left a mark. She hoped he left proof they'd broken Ben's rules to be together tonight. The pace he set was slow, and he pulled his finger all the way out each time before he shoved it deep again. She was already so freaking close, but this wasn't enough. Not nearly enough.

"I want more," she huffed in a shaky whisper.

"This is enough for tonight."

Annalise reared back and searched his face. Confusion washed over his features briefly before realization settled in his striking green eyes. "You don't think you'll ever see me again," he murmured in a deep timbre her heart had already memorized.

Exactly that. She was scared. Terrified that this...tonight...was all they had for the rest of their lives. She couldn't bring herself to say her fears out loud though, so she kissed him instead, silently pleading for him to give her more.

"Fuck," he murmured against her lips. And then she was moving again. He lifted her off the hood of his truck and settled her on the ground. The grass tickled her shoulder blades, but he'd found a soft enough spot. Jaxon was in work mode right now, on his knees between her legs, pulling her shorts and panties off with a look of such intensity, her stomach dropped to her back. He was beautiful, if a man could be called that. Tall and strong, his wide shoulders and arms flexing with every movement, his jaw gritted in fierce determination, his gaze between her legs with that striking shifter color glowing from them. Now she could see his tattoos weren't just on his neck and arms, but covered his chest as well. Whoever had done them was a true artist. They'd turned his body into a canvas, into a masterpiece. His black hair was mussed from removing his shirt, and the moonlight cast his muscles in shadows and highlights that made her wish she had a camera to capture this moment.

Even with the animal snarl in his throat and those inhuman eyes, he was perfect.

She reached for him, needing suddenly to touch his smooth skin again, needing for him to be pressed against her. He was so much bigger than her, but she felt safe, even as he crushed his weight on top of her and kissed her hard. Before She-Devil, it would've been too rough, but now she was purring that he wasn't being gentle. His hand went to the back of her head, and he gripped her hair and arched her head back, exposing her neck to his biting kisses again. And then he was there, the head of his cock touching her entrance. Her reaction was to claw her fingers up his back.

Stomach flexing against hers, Jaxon slid into her, inch by inch, until she was filled with him. So big. Almost too much. Annalise let off a low groan at how good it felt to have him finally inside her. He held there, buried deep, teeth on her neck, before he eased out again. His lips went to hers on the next stroke, and this thrust was harder, and the next was even harder, faster. His control was slipping, and she fucking loved it. His hands were tight in her hair, and rough on her back as he dragged her even closer. He was pumping into her so fast now, so smooth, hips slamming against hers. It was hard to breathe he was so heavy, so all-encompassing, but panic never made an appearance. All she felt was adored and safe as he guided them both closer to climax. Hips bucking, Jaxon pushed up on his locked arms and told her, "Watch me, Anna." He gritted his teeth and slammed into her again. "Watch me come. Watch what you do to me."

His abs flexed every time he pushed into her, his triceps bulged from where he strained above her, and she'd never seen a sexier man than this one, rutting, slamming into her, his eyes locked fiercely on hers.

Annalise cried out his name as her orgasm exploded around him. He slid deep into her and then froze as a feral snarl ripped from him. He dropped down to her again, and his teeth were in this kiss, unforgiving, biting, on the verge of drawing blood as he thrust into her again. His dick throbbed inside of her, filling her with streams of warmth, over and over, encouraging her aftershocks to match his. This was everything. It was the biggest high, the warmest warmth, the deepest feeling, the most soul-consuming sensation. She'd never experienced anything like this.

Jaxon's grip gentled in her hair as he slowed his pace, and then he stopped moving completely, other than to massage the back of her neck. His breath tickled her throat as he petted her, adored her. Encouraged by his open affection, she ran her nails lightly up and down the strong planes of his back until the growl in his throat died completely.

After minutes of silence, he murmured, "I didn't like that."

Annalise froze, her fingers mid-stroke on his shoulder blades. "Being with me?"

"No, woman. I mean, I didn't like you being scared you would never see me again. It got me riled up and...well...I was going to try and take it slower with you."

"Oh," she said, filled with potent relief. "Well, I don't know if you knew this, but I'm a floozy."

"Stop," he said, chuckling.

"It's true. These granny panties attract a lot of flies to this honey pot."

"Oh, my God," he muttered, rolling off her. "That's an awful visual." He had pulled her with him, though, and tucked her right against his side. He rested his head on his free arm and stared up at the stars. "Texting you but never seeing you was really hard," he admitted low. "Sometimes I would go crazy on those days we would rile each other up, when you would talk dirty, and I would want to touch you and be in you so fucking bad I couldn't think about anything else. It wasn't just that I wanted your body, Anna. You got me addicted to you. Seeing your messages first thing in the morning got me hooked on that feeling of waking up to you. And when I was having a shit day and you would send me a picture of what you were eating or doing, I would imagine I was with you, not dealing with the shit storm that was my life. I hated not being able to hear your voice, but I don't have great control over my animal, and I knew I would give myself away."

"Same here. I tried to convince myself you weren't real and we weren't going anywhere. I knew we were stagnant, but I was okay with that because my whole life was stagnant. It was all I could ask for. Jaxon, I'm sorry."

He swallowed audibly in the dim moonlight. "Okay, tell me why."

"For keeping my panther a secret, also for ending

us like I did. I shouldn't have told you I was moving in with someone else. I should've been woman enough to tell you what was really happening."

"Don't waste headspace on guilt, Anna. I lied right along with you. I'm sorry, too."

"I have regrets, but my biggest one? Jax, I went crazy and dropped my phone in water to cut myself off from the temptation."

"You can get a new phone."

"Yeah, but I lost all of our text conversations." Her voice broke on the last word and she hated how weak she sounded. "Those were my happy place. I liked re-reading old conversations when I was down. I needed a complete re-do if I was going to get some kind of normal life back, but cutting myself off from you hurt way worse than I expected it to. I don't read books. I never have, but I would spend nights scrolling through our old texts and just smiling and laughing my head off. Our story is my favorite story."

"Is that why you came to the Red Havoc Crew? To start over?"

She nodded once and propped her cheek on her palm, her elbow on the grass so she could see his face better when she tried to explain. "I know nothing,

Jaxon. Like…She-Devil has lighter spots in her coat, like a leopard, where most of the other panthers here are solid black. I have no idea what that even means. I might be a freak. I don't recognize myself anymore. There's nothing left of the old me. I have no control and was locking myself in a cage-room when I felt like I would shift, just to protect the outside world from myself."

"You call your animal She-Devil?" he asked softly, looking down at her.

She cuddled closer against his side and nodded. "She's a beast. I think she needs a crew. Or at the very least people around who can stop me if I get out of control."

"So, you're putting yourself in another cage. Out here."

She hadn't thought of it that way, but yeah, kind of. "The crew might be the bars of my cage now, but at least it feels more like freedom."

Jaxon sighed and rested his chin on top of her head. "You need Red Havoc?"

Heart aching, she nodded. "I think so."

His heartbeat was racing under her hand as he whispered, "Then we'll get you Red Havoc." It sounded like an oath. Like a promise to keep her safe and secure, what she needed. But she knew that meant he wouldn't be in the picture, and right now, that was unimaginable.

"Don't leave," she pleaded. "I need the cage, but I don't want to be alone again."

"You'll have your crew—"

"You keep me steady. It's different with Ben and the boys. Sometimes they make me feel worse. Like I have less control. And I'm so lonely, Jax. Please. Stay here, and we can sneak and see each other while I learn about this...this...*thing* that I am. Stay for a few days."

"You want me to be your secret?" he asked. She didn't miss the hurt that tainted his voice.

"Until Ben gets over whatever prejudice he has against outside shifters. I just...I don't know what I'm doing, but when I'm touching you, I feel like everything is going to be okay somehow."

"It will be okay," he promised, his deep voice steady. Truth. He truly believed it. "I'll stay in town and make sure you get settled here. And when I know you're safe and happy, I'll go."

Her mind skittered away from the pain those last

two words inflicted on her heart, so she decided to ignore that part. That was the boring part she was going to try to figure out a way to get rid of.

She didn't know how yet, but she was going to shake things up in Red Havoc because Annalise needed both the panthers and Jaxon now. She needed moments like these where she was wrapped up with a man who made her feel whole and okay just the way she was, as well as the crew who would push her to become a better version of herself, and stronger.

So, okay. He could pretend he was going to leave. But already She-Devil had plans on sinking her claws in deeper to the man who had won her heart before she'd even heard his voice.

FIVE

Jaxon knelt at the edge of the tree line and watched Anna make her way carefully down the deer trail. Watching her leave made it hard for him to draw a breath, so he gripped his shirt over his chest and forced air into his lungs despite the ache. What had she done? Everything in him wanted to cross panther territory lines and drag her back to his truck, buckle her up inside, and drive her away from here.

If he was honest, he wanted to fucking kidnap her like a psychopath. She was a panther, and she belonged with a panther crew, but inside, his bear was roaring that she belonged with him, and fuck her people.

He could always kill them. The thought crossed

his mind earlier today, and then again tonight when she'd admitted she had to stay here. The selfish monster inside of him wanted to cut off anyone who could take her from him.

But then she'd said she needed the cage Red Havoc could provide, and it had shifted something inside of him. He didn't know what it was like for a bitten shifter, but if she was scared of herself, scared of the animal inside of her, well…he did understand that. And now he felt like he would sacrifice just about anything to make sure she got control of her animal. Because her voice had gone empty and hollow when she'd talked about the cage room, and about her old life. And he would be good-goddamned if he was going to let her ever feel that kind of loneliness again.

Pairing up with a woman wasn't supposed to be like this.

He was selfish by nature and had been wanting a mate. A human mate so that he could fuck her, care about her well-being, but not bond to her like with a shifter female. He wanted to pretend he wasn't this *thing* and live a normal human life with a human wife. He wanted to ignore the bear. He wanted to

Change in the woods in private a few times a month and the rest of the time pretend he'd been born a normal man, not a Gray Back.

Annalise called herself She-Devil. Well, his bear was named Titan, something he wouldn't admit too soon so she wouldn't get scared. If she knew what kind of hellish revenge his inner grizzly was plotting on the entirety of the Red Havoc Crew, she would understand why he was rogue and run away from him screaming. And what had the crew done wrong? Not a goddamn thing. They only existed as a barrier between him and something Titan wanted—Annalise.

Her admitting she needed to be a part of this crew, without Jaxon, had done something incredible to his human side. It had made him want to help her, settle her here, and give her a good life. But it had also done something awful to the bear. It made him want to draw her in close and burn the world around them until she had nothing left but him.

He should leave.

She wants us to stay.

Jaxon shook his head and ran his hands through his hair roughly. Fucking Titan. Manipulative, like always.

Down the trail, Annalise turned and gave him a shy smile and a little wave. Beautiful. She was so much prettier than he'd imagined. She had dark brunette hair. He'd yanked her hair band out just to free her tresses and see them waving past her shoulders. Soft as silk, shiny in the moonlight. Even from here he could see the pretty gold in her panther eyes and her stark freckles she'd once told him she didn't like. Crazy girl. Those little dots all over her face were so fucking cute he couldn't stand it. Maybe that's why she had spots in her coat.

He nodded to her just before she turned and disappeared down the trail. Already he missed her. God, he was losing his mind.

Bring her back.

Jaxon shook his head hard. *Shut the fuck up, Titan. She belongs here.*

A wave of nausea threatened to make him gag on that thought, and before he could stop Titan's imaginings, a picture of them driving from town to town flashed through his mind. Endless road trips, her smiling from the passenger's seat of his truck, and him fucking her relentlessly in cheap motels. But Titan had made a misstep with that image. What kind of life would that be for a girl like Annalise? She'd come here to settle. She wasn't a nomad, and if she said her cat needed a crew, she sure as hell wasn't a rogue.

Jaxon was stuck in an endless cycle of roaming and spending a few days with the Gray Backs. Roaming, Gray Backs, roaming, Gray Backs, times infinity. He couldn't stop. He'd tried and failed a hundred times.

Titan would ruin Annalise. Her cat needed stability, and all he had to offer was chaos.

He muttered a curse and stood, made his way to his truck, shaking his head. When he looked up to grab the door handle, Ben stood there against the door of his ride, arms crossed, eyes blazing gold, lips curled back to expose teeth that were too sharp at the canines.

Jaxon startled hard and skidded to a stop. Damn cats could sneak up on anyone. It made him want to bleed the alpha. Typical Titan.

"Move," he rumbled in warning.

To Jaxon's utter surprise, Ben did. Immediately. Jaxon narrowed his eyes suspiciously and climbed into his truck, but Ben slid into the passenger's seat and demanded, "Drive, Grizzly."

Now Jaxon didn't like being told what to do in general—that was the Gray Back in him—but he was pretty damn close to panther territory and Ben had control over Annalise's future. Not bothering to hide the growl in his throat, Jaxon hit the gas and eased them onto the abandoned logging road he'd found earlier.

"I forbade her to see you, and you have her breaking my rules immediately." Ben's voice shook with fury.

"If you Change in my truck, we're going to have a huge problem," Jaxon warned him.

"What is it about her? What do you want with her?"

"She ain't your cat yet."

Ben slammed his open palm against the dashboard. "I lost two already! In a year, I've lost two, Grizzly. You are rogue. You aren't an alpha, so you can't understand what it does to a man like me to lose crew. I want her."

Red rage boiled up through Jaxon's chest, and he slammed on the brakes so hard the truck skidded sideways before it lurched to a stop. "What the fuck do you mean, you want her?"

"I'm paired up. Bonded. I have my family built. I don't have a complete crew yet, though. My animal...I need more. I need Annalise under me."

"Great. If that's what she wants, I'm good with it. So why the fuck are you telling me this."

"Because tonight I got a call from someone I haven't spoken to in a lot of years, someone who changed my life when I was a cub. Someone who told me before I went into Apex, and before my panther got stripped from my body, that I would get my animal back someday. Someone who can see the future, gave me hope, and got me through that goddamned facility on the days when I just wanted to give up."

"Beaston," Jaxon murmured. Why was Beaston involved in this now?

"Yeah. Him. The seer from your crew called me and told me I have to let Annalise go. And when I asked him why? He said one word before he hung up."

"What word?"

"Jaxon."

"Jesus," Jaxon uttered on a breath. So she was it

then. Annalise was his. A mixture of relief and utter disappointment spun inside of him like a slow-moving tornado. Relief because she felt important, and if Beaston said she was his, then she was, and that was that. But nothing had changed over the past few hours. He was still a nomad, still a rogue, and would still hurt Annalise and She-Devil with the life he required to stay steady.

"Why couldn't you have just left her alone?" Ben said quietly. He didn't smell of rage anymore, and the raw waves of power weren't pulsing from the alpha's body any longer. He sounded defeated.

"How did you lose your cats?"

Ben twitched his head and made a ticking sound behind his teeth. "None of your business, Outsider."

In this moment, Ben reminded Jaxon so much of the alpha he'd grown up under, Creed. He was strong, firm, but quiet with the hard stuff, and never let outsiders know about the inner workings of his crew. So he waited. Time was the only thing that had ever loosened up Creed, and the same worked here in the dark woods that bordered Red Havoc territory, in his truck, with the sound of the dinging seatbelt warning the only noise to break up the heavy silence.

At last, Ben murmured, "I had a female named Winter. I worked on her for three years to pledge, but she never attached. It was a failure. She fit here, and I couldn't get her to commit. I had to let her go find a better life in Kane's Blackwing Crew. It ripped my guts out to say goodbye, knowing I was really letting her go to another alpha. To a crew who weren't panthers. I've had to put down cats before. It changes an alpha's soul when you can't fix one, when the only help you can offer is ending their suffering and protecting the world from the poisoned animal inside of them. Those kills are dark marks against your soul. And saying goodbye to Winter felt just as awful. I thought that was the worst it could get."

"Who was the second cat?"

"A panther named Brody. He was the reason for Winter leaving, and then seven months back, he up and left his mate, right after she'd given him a cub. He left me. He left the crew. And then he did something terrible."

Dread dumped into Jaxon as a sudden, horrifying instinct reared its head. "What kind of something terrible?"

Ben rolled his head against the headrest and

leveled Jaxon with a dead-eyed stare. "Brody is a rare one. He's a black leopard. He had spots in his coat."

Now it was Jaxon who wanted to slam his hand on the dashboard. He almost didn't want to hear the rest. He wanted to kick the alpha out and drive back down to Ben's little Po-Dunk moonshine camp and load Annalise in his truck and take her far away from here. But he needed to know about the fucker he was about to start hunting. "What did he do?" he gritted out through clenched teeth as he strangled the steering wheel.

Ben inhaled deeply. "Brody Turned Annalise into a panther. She won't talk to me about it. She refuses, so I know it was bad. Brody ruined that girl's life. The blood he spilled, the pain he caused, and that wild animal constantly snarling to rip out of her skin? That's on me because Brody was my crew, and I lost control of him."

Realization slammed into Jaxon's chest. "That's why you really need her. Redemption."

"You can't be a part of my crew, Grizzly. Not ever. I won't allow it."

"I don't want to be a member of your little kitty-squad, asshole."

Ben scratched his jaw in an irritated gesture. "The Gray Backs have the best trackers in the world."

"Yeah, including me."

"You learned from Beaston? From Bash? From your dad?"

Jaxon dipped his chin once.

"I can't find Brody," Ben admitted quietly.

Jaxon huffed a pissed-off breath, slammed his head back against the headrest, and stared out into the woods illuminated by his headlights. "You won't let me near Annalise, but you want to use me to avenge her. I don't need a kill mission from you, Panther. I was already going after him."

"Bring him to me alive, and we'll talk about Annalise's future."

"No deal. She belongs with you. I'll kill the fucker, slowly like my animal requires, and I'll bring you proof. And then you let Annalise into your crew because she told me something tonight that put me out of the running."

"What did she tell you?"

"That her animal needs something steady."

"And that's not you?"

Jaxon shook his head, wishing to God he was

different. That he was better. That he was worthy of a woman like Annalise. "Not even close. Last name."

"Brakeen."

"Last place you tracked Brody Brakeen to?"

"South Dakota. Annalise lived in St. Louis, though. I think the bite happened there, but it was six months back. He could be anywhere."

"What happened to his mate and cub?" Jaxon asked, feeling sick to his stomach.

Ben shoved the door open and got out. And right before he slammed it, he said, "Lynn is Red Havoc business."

Jaxon didn't miss the anger that flashed across his face, though. It wasn't the anguished expression that would tell him the female panther wasn't walking the earth anymore. It was a reaction that told Jaxon she was probably spiraling because of what Brody had done.

Three women hurt—some female named Winter, Brody's mate, Lynn, and now Annalise. Brody was a beast—a destroyer of bonds, a creator of monsters. He was a life-ruiner. A woman-ruiner who left a trail of shattered hearts in his wake. Turning someone against their will was the biggest law broken in his world. It created shifters like Annalise, whose animal had been born in violence and would never be easy to manage. It created shifters who had to be put down if they weren't strong enough to control the volatile animals inside of them. It created She-Devils.

This was it. This was the hunt his bear lived for. Blood for a cause. Blood for vengeance. Blood for justice.

It would be the most satisfying hunt of Titan's entire existence.

SIX

Jaxon Barns was sex on a stick...whatever that saying meant. Annalise adjusted the floral bag of shower stuff on her arm and switched her fluffy purple towel to her other hip as she made her way toward the communal restrooms down at the end of the row of Red Havoc cabins. Her flipflops clacked loudly with each step, echoing across the empty clearing.

She couldn't stop thinking about the way he'd touched her last night. The way it had felt like a match carelessly flicked into a puddle of gasoline the second their bodies had collided in that soul-altering embrace. Making out on the hood of his truck and his hand down the front of her shorts. She'd woken up way too early feeling feverish to see him again. Not just for sex, but for that high of feeling safe around him.

"You're thinking about the grizzly," Jenny said, appearing right beside Annalise.

Annalise startled hard and skittered to the side. She didn't often get snuck up on now that She-Devil existed and paid attention to everything.

She gave Jenny a sideways glance and steadied out her pace again. The alpha's mate had her dark hair piled up in a messy bun on top of her head, not a stich of make-up on, and she still somehow managed to look glamorous. Annalise was all baggy sweat pants, a tank top that was too long, and looked exactly as though she'd only slept fitfully for three hours last night. That part was the fault of Jaxon and her perverted mind that kept swirling around the sexy way his abs had flexed against her stomach every time he pumped his dick deeper into her.

"N-no, I'm not thinking about him."

"Your pants are in serious danger of catching fire there, Annalise. Even if I couldn't hear the stutter or the false notes in your voice"—Jenny pointed to Annalise's face—"you're stroking your lips like a weirdo."

Oh, God, she really was. She yanked her hand from her mouth.

"Ben busted you two last night, just so you know you didn't get away with anything. He sees everything that happens in and near his territory." Jenny arched her delicate eyebrows high and gave her a serious look. "Careful with the grizzly. Ben and the boys can't handle other dominants in their territory, and I don't know if your instincts are firing on all pistons yet, but your boyfriend? He's a frickin' monster. It's like a wasp in a hive, girl. You don't want to get these boys all riled up. You're gonna get blood on their hands if you aren't more careful."

"Jaxon was defending himself just fine yesterday," Annalise muttered, feeling defensive.

"Oooh," Jenny drawled out. "He has a name to you. So real feelings attached, too?" Jenny hugged her white towel to her chest and shook her head. "You're gonna give my mate gray hairs prematurely. I'm calling it now. You'll be worse than Lynn."

Annalise cast a quick glance back toward the cabins sitting quietly in the gray dawn light in the shadow of the Appalachian Mountains. "Which house does she live in?"

"None of them right now. She's in the treehouse. Lynn has some stuff she's working through, but if she comes back to us, she'll live there." Jenny pointed behind them to the cabin right next to Annalise's, second from the front.

Well, okay. Maybe Lynn was crazy, but Annalise was actually relieved that there might eventually be another girl in the crew. "Admission," Annalise said softly as she pulled open the door to the bathroom, which looked like a little log cabin. "I don't have any girl-friends anymore."

"Welcome to the club," Jenny said, pulling a toothbrush from the bag on her shoulder. "That's one of the pitfalls of getting your ass bitten by a panther shifter. Girls are harder to come by in the big cat community. It's a boys' club. Sometimes the ladies don't make very good monsters, if you know what I mean."

"Yeah, actually, I completely get what you're saying. I make a terrible monster."

"Oh, my God, the worst," Jenny said with a giggle as she started brushing her teeth at the sink. Around a frothy mouth of toothpaste, she said, "I saw your claw marks on Barret's face, remember? Those were deep and intentional. You went after your own people and gave your back to a Gray Back grizzly. You're crazy."

Annalise's frown deepened so much it made her forehead hurt. "Thanks."

"Lynn's crazy, too, and so am I, so don't get your panties in a twist. You're a black leopard, right?"

That question left Annalise completely baffled. "No. I'm a panther."

"Yeah, but there are two kinds of big cats that fall under the panther shifter category. Get it? *Cat-egory?*" Jenny spat toothpaste in the sink and dipped down to fill her mouth straight from the faucet. She gurgled, spat again, and then said, "I saw your spots. We've only had one black leopard in the crew before, and he was a douche-canoe of the highest level. I'm a Jaguar. The boys are all Jaguars too, and so is Lynn. All black big-cats are called Panthers. But you're a rare one, Miss Ma'am."

Huh. Well that actually answered a burning question she'd had about her spots. Cool. A black leopard. "Can I play twenty questions?"

"Let me guess," Jenny said, making her way into

one of the shower stalls. "The boys haven't explained anything to you."

"I asked questions the first couple days but gave up when Anson answered everything with 'your momma.'"

"Ha!" Jenny blasted out a laugh that echoed through the bathroom. "And asking Greyson would've gotten you the silent treatment. And Barret would've probably just tried to bite you. That man is a savage. Did you ask Ben anything?"

"No." Annalise made her way into a stall of her own and pulled the curtain closed. Living out here was like living at a campground, and as she watched a spider drag its waterlogged body across the shower floor toward the drain, she thought perhaps she would never get used to this. "Ben feels big. It's hard to explain. It's like, when I'm around him, it's hard to breathe and my chest gets all tight and my panther wants to rip out of my skin and fight him."

The water turned on in Jenny's stall. "Good God, you really are crazy. The first part of your story was normal. That heaviness you feel from Ben? That's his alpha mojo. You *should* feel that. That's what he uses to control the crew. Sounds bad, but they need all the guidance Ben can give them. He collects the broken souls, the C-Teamers, the big cats no one else wants. Some crews live closer to civilization, but we live out here for a reason. This place is Ben's attempt to rehabilitate problem shifters."

Annalise stripped out of her clothes and turned on the water as hot as it would go. "Well, that's noble of him. I guess that's why he is fine with me here." Honestly, she didn't really like that she'd been let into Red Havoc territory because she was broken.

The sound of a shampoo bottle popped, and then Jenny called over the wall, "It's more noble than you understand."

"What do you mean?" Annalise asked, stepping under the steaming jets of water.

"Alphas who take the broken ones risk having to put them down. Some can't be saved."

Gooseflesh rippled across her skin, and Annalise froze. "What do you mean 'put them down?'"

"You know what I mean. We police ourselves outside of human law. Sometimes killing is necessary."

"No, no, no, it's never necessary because that's murder, and murder is wrong."

"That's the human in you talking. Listen to your panther, though. She'll see the necessity in killing off the dangerous ones."

"Well, she thinks it's a great idea to kill everything that breathes, so she's not really who I go to for life-advice. Oh, my God, Ben kills people?"

"You'll kill someday, too."

Horrible memories of the night she'd been Turned washed through her mind like a tsunami, and Annalise closed her eyes against the onslaught. No one could know what really happened that night. "That's why I came here, so that I wouldn't go all kitty-serial-killer on the outside world. Ben is supposed to stop me, or protect everyone from me, or something. But he's a killer!"

Jenny sighed a tired sound. "Annalise, your life is different now. You'll have to learn how to let your old life and your old views go. Shifters go to war, shifters fight over territory, humans try to hurt and expose us and have to be dealt with. There's always something happening. It's just the way it is."

"But I never saw anything about this online or in the news."

"And you won't if we're handling things correctly.

What would you have Ben do with a panther who goes on a killing spree? Women, children, he just goes mad, and his animal takes over and ends human lives. Hmm? What would you have him do with that shifter?"

"Give them to the police!"

"So they can lock him up with other people, who he would kill or Turn into a monster shifter, just like him."

Damn. Jenny had a point. "Isn't there some shifter maximum security prison or something?"

"Yes," Jenny murmured softly over the sound of running water. "And putting down the unsalvageable shifters is a kindness to them, Annalise. Ben doesn't do it lightly. He saves who he can, and when he has to make the hard decisions, it rips him up inside. For always. He's no killer. He's an alpha, and they have to keep their crews, as well as the outside world, safe. You shouldn't ever give into your urge to fight him, Annalise. Challenging an alpha is a really bad idea and can get you killed. Don't push him to make an example of you. Don't force his hand. If he goes easy on you, the boys will start challenging him for alpha, and it will be chaos in the crew. There are no submissives here, and everything hangs in a very fine balance. Don't fuck with that balance. It wouldn't take much to poison this crew. You want to fight someone? Go after Barret. He's Second and a total dick ninety-four percent of the time. Plus it would be hilarious if he lost Second to a girl."

"Wait, why aren't you Second? You're Ben's mate."

Jenny snorted. "Not how it works, Newbie. I had to fight for my place at the bottom of the crew. I care nothing for dominance and crew politics. I only care about if Ben and Raif are happy."

"I have to admit, you coming out of the trees yesterday with that rifle like some zombie-slaying badass was pretty cool," Annalise said, scrubbing shampoo into her hair.

"Flattery will get you everywhere with me. You and the boys were a mess yesterday. I wanted it done and the grizzly out of our territory. He's bad news. All Gray Backs are."

"Why?"

"Because they are notoriously violent monster beasties, and I like survival. You can't trust a Gray Back. They're the original C-Team. Creed is like Ben and collected a menagerie of broken shifters, then tried to make them get along. Except rumor has it they fight all the damn time. Think what you did yesterday, going after your own crew, and multiply that by entire crew battles, just ripping each other to shreds for fun. And you brought a mother-fucking Barns into Red Havoc territory. His daddy, Matt, is this scarred-up beast bear who survived years in some testing facility. And his momma? Willamena Mother-Freakin' Madden, now Barns. She's a worm-loving weirdo. Glasses, dyed red hair, little, compact, doesn't look like she could lift a can of beans out of the pantry. But she was Turned by Beaston, the monster of monsters, and the moment her grizzly comes out, she brings hell. She's one of the only female shifters to take Second in a crew, and she's dominant over all those broken Gray Backs. Except for Creed. She and Matt made little monster babies, who grew up to be demon grizzlies, and you brought one here, to a crew already on shaky ground."

Oh, she hadn't just brought Jaxon here. She'd totally had a diddle party with him up on the mountain last night. Standing here under the hot jets of shower water, she waited for regrets that didn't come. What Jenny was telling her should've scared her, but it didn't. She knew Jaxon. Knew him from months of texting and building a tentative bond already. He might attack every last one of the Red Havoc Crew, she didn't know, but in her heart she *did* know he would be protective of her. And yeah, maybe he was a demon grizzly, but he hadn't hurt her during the fight yesterday, even when she gave him her back. And he hadn't hurt her last night during boink-apalooza. He'd given her the epic fucking of her lifetime, plus one billion butterflies in her stomach.

Maybe her instincts really were broken. She-Devil practically purred inside of her every time she thought about Jaxon. Grizzly or no, he felt important, and she wanted more time with him. She knew it was wrong to be with Jaxon, but hadn't figured out why yet. And the why it was wrong was the most important question.

"Jenny?"

"Yeah?"

"Why aren't panthers allowed to mix with other shifters?"

Jenny sighed. "That's a question with a layered answer. The biggest one is that we're rare. If you and

Jaxon had a cub, there's a fifty percent chance you would be having a grizzly. There's plenty of those. Also, the mixed crews get a lot of attention. They're out to the public and proud. People take their pictures and want their autographs. They are recognized wherever they go. But big cat shifters tend to stay to themselves in prides or crews because our animals have the instinct to band together and stay hidden and safe. Panthers have always stuck with panthers. It's just the way it is. We can't bring in a grizzly like Jaxon, Annalise. Ben would have trouble holding the crew. That man is too dominant, and his animal too big. He would turn this crew into the blood-letting Gray Backs within days. He would ruin Red Havoc and everything we've built." Jenny turned off the water, and Annalise heard her shove the curtain aside. "You could've been with him if you were anything but a panther, Annalise. But that's life. That's shifter life. It isn't fair. Protect your crew and let him go."

Jenny's flip flops clacked on the tile as she made her way to the door. With the barrier shut behind the woman, and Annalise left alone in the bathroom, the loneliness in her chest threatened to overwhelm her.

It was like the old days when she'd first been Turned and had to give up all her friends for their safety. When she'd had to cut herself off from the world to protect it.

Annalise slid her back down the wall and pulled her knees against her chest, hugged them tightly, and watched the spider crawling along the wall across from her. He was going slow, impeded by the water.

She and that spider were the same—wet, alone, and dragging themselves through life.

She didn't want to be the spider anymore, though.

She wanted to create a life worth living. One where she chased smiles, got the one billion butterflies, and became a functioning member of a crew.

She wanted it all.

Now, she just needed to figure out a way to have her panther-shaped cake and eat her grizzly-shaped cake, too.

SEVEN

1. See Jaxon again asap.

2. Make him fall in love with me asap.

3. Make Ben stop being a douche-titty-kitty.

4. Make Anson and Barret stop being pecker-faces.

5. Make Greyson talk to me in more than single syllable caveman grunts.

6. Get everyone to stop calling me Princess Panther.

7. Make Jenny be my friend. And possibly Crazy Lynn?

8. Get a motherfuckin' job. Maybe this should be number 3.

9. Steal a car to get me to the super-awesome job I find.

10. Call Samuel so he doesn't worry.
11. Find a magical serum to cure shifter-dom, aka kill She-Devil.
12. Marry Jaxon and have a dozen of his monster bear-panther babies.
13. Live happily ever after in the woods with a bunch of gross boys who I'm pretty sure are making moonshine on the mountain behind my cabin.

Annalise giggled as she finished writing the last word of her list into her notebook with a flourish of her ballpoint pen. Some of these were jokes. For example, she didn't really want a dozen babies. Four would be fine. And she probably wouldn't do any grand theft auto. She had some money saved for an old beater car if she could get a good deal.

She'd always been a list maker, but over the past six months, she'd gotten overwhelmed and stopped doing the things that used to bring her joy. This list was a way to meet short-term goals one by one until she got to the big goal—happiness. She wanted that really bad, but this morning in the shower, as she'd watched that pitiful spider, she'd realized that happiness wasn't just going to fall into her lap if she pouted long enough about her lousy lot in life. Happiness was something she was going to have to work to create.

Movement out the front window caught her attention, and she stood in a rush to find Greyson walking past her cabin. Yes! Gripping her notebook to her ample teets, she made her way outside and called from the top step of her porch, "Hi Greyson!"

He ignored her like a champ.

"Lovely weather we're having today, isn't it?"

Her cave man grunted. Getting warmer.

"What are you up to today? Where are you headed?" she called louder as he strode toward the side of her house. Greyson turned like he was going to answer, and she poised to mark number five off the list. But instead of saying an actual word, he lifted his middle finger and glared at her instead, then disappeared around the corner. Lovely.

She nearly tripped over a box sitting on the second to top stairs when she strode down to go find Anson to pester him into liking her. With a frown, she bent down, picked it up, and shook it gently. It was covered in clear masking tape. There were probably a dozen layers of it, and when she turned it around in her hands, there were words written on the side in dark marker.

Use your claws.
-Jax

Frantically, she scanned the clearing in front of her cabin, but she was alone. How had he snuck up here to deliver this without being caught by Ben, who apparently magically knew everything that happened in his territory? She was calling bullcaca on Jenny's claim. She had no doubt now that Jaxon could come and go as he pleased, and not get caught if he didn't want to. Sexy giant stalker.

Use her claws? She flicked out her fingers like wolverine, but nothing happened. "Fing," she said on the next try, but still nothing.

"I didn't mean literally, Anna," a deep rumbling voice sounded from the corner of her cabin.

She screeched and skidded down the stairs, then landed hard on her butt on the very bottom one. The box landed in the dirt in front of her.

"Oh, my God, how have you survived up until

now," Jaxon said from right beside her.

He reached out to help her up, but she swatted away his giant paw and scrambled upright. "You're supposed to ask if I'm okay after you put me on the ground."

"I didn't do that. You should've heard me coming. Can you not smell me, woman?"

"Well…" She sniffed delicately. It did smell heavily of Jaxon's cologne and his bear's fur. "Maybe I was distracted by presents and riddles."

"Were you trying to make your claws come out of your human fingers?" he asked. "Because you can't."

Damn his amused smile, she wanted to claw that off. "You're making me mad. And a little embarrassed. I thought for a second you meant I could be a badass like Cat Woman and just…make my weapons come out."

"Speaking of your weapons." Jaxon turned around and pulled his blue and black plaid lumberjack shirt up, along with his black T-shirt, and exposed two sets of angry-looking claw marks that were practically healed already.

She canted her head and tried to contain her smile. "If you're waiting for an apology, I'm not sorry."

"You remember that conversation?" he asked low as he settled his shirts back into place and leaned against the railing of her porch. That sexy man felt a dozen feet tall and nearly blocked out the damn sun behind him with his wide shoulders.

"Of course I remember. I have a bad habit of thinking I'm always doing the wrong thing, and so I apologize for things that I shouldn't."

"The first time you apologized, I was so confused. I was busy working. It was a bad day for the family business. A bad day for the Gray Backs, too. A bunch of shipments got messed up, and it brought angry humans into Damon's Mountains. I was working to fix the mistakes, trying to keep some of the grizzlies from going territorial on the humans. I didn't have time to breathe all day, much less look at my phone. I thought about you, but I just couldn't get a second to text you during the chaos. It was bad. And when we finally got everything settled down, I went straight back to my trailer and checked my messages. There were a ton from you. They started out so cute. I was smiling because it felt so fucking good to read about your normal day when I'd just spent hours trying to keep Beaston and Jason and my dad from maiming some pissed-off humans. You'd taken a picture at a coffee shop of this mug that said *You're Hot*. You took me shopping, took pictures and messaged me, and you went to the post office and took a selfie of this stuffed valentine's bear. *Aaand* that's when it hit me what day it was. February fourteenth, and my head had been so messed up since first thing that morning, I hadn't realized the holiday. Your messages got worried. You asked if I was okay. There were a couple hours of silence, and then you apologized for bothering me." Jaxon's dark eyebrows lowered, and he shook his head. "As if you could bother me, Anna. Your messages were the best part of my day. I felt bad for not wishing you a happy Valentine's Day, and I felt frustrated you thought you had to apologize for something so silly."

"Yeah," she murmured, remembering the pain of uncertainty that day. "I was hoping you would do something sweet, or send me a video and ask me to be your valentine. Totally lame, I know, but I was also depending on you for normal. And you were gentle but firm and told me to never apologize for anything unless I actually did something wrong. And for the rest of that night, I felt like I'd gotten in trouble by you."

"I could tell. You got quiet, and when I messaged you asking if you were okay, you texted back *I'm fine*." Jaxon stepped forward, brushed his hands through her hair, and cupped the back of her head, angled her face up toward him. "When my dad asks my ma that, and she answers 'I'm fine,' my brother, Jathan, and I always knew to get the hell out of dodge, because she would eventually explode and rip my dad a new asshole." The corner of his lip curved up slightly in a smile that disappeared when he began talking again. "I waited for you to rip me, but you didn't. You just got more quiet. For a couple of days, I was afraid I'd lost you, and I couldn't understand why. I had all these visions of having to wake up without your messages, to go through my day not talking to you, and it sucked. I wasn't ready to lose you. I even thought about calling you."

"Wow, that's some desperation. An actual phone call, Jax? You *must've* been scared."

He chuckled and drew closer to her, massaging the back of her head gently with his fingertips. His eyes were striking in the saturated sunlight as he studied her face. They were caught between his human caramel brown and the green of his animal, and they glowed from the pupils out, ever so slightly. "I begged you to talk to me. To tell me what was wrong."

"I needed time because I didn't like getting in trouble for something I was already self-conscious about. I knew I had a problem with apologizing. Every boyfriend I've ever had has made a comment about how they hated that I did that. It was my go-to reaction for everything. I was mad that you'd pointed it out so early in the relationship we were building, and you weren't even physically around me to hear me apologizing. You saw that about me too soon. I felt exposed and scared of what we were becoming and angry at myself for not having fixed that habit before. And when I explained it, you were so sweet, so understanding, but still firm in telling me I needed to work on it for me, not for you or for anyone else. But you said you wanted to see me strong, not groveling, not taking my reactions back, not saying sorry for things I shouldn't feel any guilt over. And so from then on, I actually worked on it."

"And now?" he asked, lifting his chin proudly as

he looked down at her.

"Now, I'm not sorry."

"That's my girl," he growled. Jaxon leaned down and kissed her. It was soft at first, his lips moving against hers with gentle ease. His tongue brushed against her bottom lip, and she opened just enough for him to slip inside of her mouth. Jaxon angled his face the other way and dragged her closer until their bodies pressed against each other. His tongue drove deeper and harder, and his hands went rough in her hair, causing a helpless whimper to crawl up the back of her throat. She clung to him, gathered the soft fabric of his outer shirt in her clenched hands to keep him close. The cat inside of her was letting off a soft growl with every breath she took, but she didn't care about that so much right now. Not when Jaxon was growling, too. Not when he was gripping the back of her neck and sliding his other hand around her back, pulling her so tight against him as if he never wanted to let her go again.

"That's enough," Ben called in a pissed-off tone, one that made Annalise wince and her inner panther hiss in defense.

Jaxon huffed an angry-sounding snarl but didn't

stop kissing her. If anything, his lips were more urgent against hers.

"Hands off my panther, Grizzly!" Ben yelled.

Jaxon ripped away from her kiss with a feral sound, and he rounded on the alpha. "Go ahead and call her yours again. I fuckin' dare you."

"Jaxon," she whispered, tugging his hand. This couldn't go to battle. They would hurt each other, and already She-Devil was snarling to escape her skin. She would hurt Ben, too, and Jenny's words about how easily this crew could fold were pounding against her skull. She couldn't bring Red Havoc down. "Babe," she murmured, squeezing his hand and running her other palm up the length of his rigid spine. "He didn't mean it like that." God, why was it so hard to breathe around him right now? It felt like a hundred pounds had just been placed on her shoulders and she was standing in quick sand, sinking inch by inch under the heavy power radiating from Jax.

Jaxon ran his hand over his hair and swallowed the snarl down. His muscles still tense under her hand, he said in a low, gravelly voice, "Best not to get Titan riled up, Panther. I was in control yesterday. It ain't always like that."

Whuuut the fuuuck? Titan? He named his damn bear, *Titan*? That was almost as bad as She-Devil.

"I invited you into my territory for a meeting," Ben growled. "Let's get this done." Ben turned on his heel and sauntered back toward his cabin. "Now, Grizzly," he barked over his shoulder.

When Annalise looked up at his face, Jaxon was smiling like a green-eyed demon, but there was no humor in the curve of his lips. There was the promise of murder. And now she was starting to understand why the boys didn't want him in their territory. Their rapport would always be like this—defensive and right on the verge of a bloodbath. The panthers were brawlers, but Jaxon's animal was different. Jenny had been right about him being too big and dominant to stay in the territory, especially with the crew on unsteady ground.

The realization blasted pain, dark and deep, through her chest. As she watched Jaxon walk away with those graceful, powerful, inhuman strides of his, she inhaled deeply, forcing her lungs to expand to ease the ache behind her sternum.

It was in this moment she realized she couldn't

have both Red Havoc and Jax.

Hands shaking from how damn close Jax and Ben had come to clawing each other, she blinked hard and picked up the box off the ground, then watched Ben open the door to his cabin and disappear inside. Jaxon hesitated on the porch, then raised those fiery green eyes to hers. She couldn't read his emotions because he'd closed down, but a strange possessiveness overtook her. Even monstrous, Jax was *hers*.

He dipped his gaze away and disappeared into Ben's house. The firm click of the door closing was loud in the silence of the clearing. And she felt alone again.

This was her least favorite feeling. It had been her only companion for months, and she was ready to move on. Ready to connect with people and build herself up again. She was ready to get out of the ashes she'd been wallowing in and be the damn phoenix already.

Just to make herself feel better, she marked off number one on her short-term goals checklist.

1. See Jaxon again asap.

Juggling her notebook and the box, she shoved

her door open and squatted down in the small living room where she didn't exactly use her claws, but she did rip and pull at that tape until she could wrestle the lid open.

Inside was a huge stack of papers. On top of the stack was a cell phone with a gold glittery case with a skull on it. There were black jewels for the skull's eyes. It was cute, and badass, and sparkly, and so her. With an emotional grin, she read the top page. He'd really done it. Jaxon had printed off all their text messages, starting from day one, when they'd found each other on that dating site and exchanged phone numbers. He'd highlighted a part of their first conversation in purple, her favorite color.

Jax: *So, you're telling me you're a girly girl then? Deal-breaker.*

Anna: *Totally girly girl. In fact, if you saw me right now, you would be appalled by my girly-ness. Guess what I'm wearing? And don't be gross about it. I'm not into dirty talk on a first text-date.*

Jax: *Okay, I've got this. You're about to be so creeped out and think I'm hiding in your bushes, looking at you through the window.*

Anna: *Hey Creepy McCreeperson, less of that.*

Jax: *Lol, okay. Pink sparkly dress, hair done up like a sixties pin-up girl, matching pink high heels, bright red lipstick, matching bejeweled phone case and purse, and because I'm a dude, I have to say I'm also imagining matching pink panties. Please say they have sequins.*

Anna: *God. I already regret giving you my number.*

Jax: *No, you don't. You like to play games. How close am I?*

Anna: *Well, I know you're not in my bushes. I just giggled saying that last part. Sounds perverted. But no. You aren't close at all. Black yoga pants, a white tank top with a mustard stain from the hot dog I ate for lunch, panties are comfy cottons in the color boring-beige, and I haven't brushed my hair in two days. Are you running yet, Jax? #girlygirl*

Jax: *#dreamgirl*

It had the times printed with the messages. It had taken Annalise three minutes to respond because he'd surprised her. She'd expected him to be turned off and leave the conversation. In a way, she'd been testing him.

Anna: *Really?*

Jax: *I'm relieved. I told you...deal breaker. I'm not really into girls who sparkle. Was I at least close on the phone case?*

Anna: *Nope. I don't even have a cute case. My phone is just black. Dream phone case would have a cute skull on it, though. I saw one once in a store. It was expensive so I didn't get it, but I still think it's the cutest one I've ever seen. I like sugar skulls.*

Annalise set the page down and ran her finger along the edge of the jewels on the phone Jax had gifted her. He'd remembered a conversation from four months ago. He'd bought her a new phone and a dream case. He didn't seem like the type of man to give gifts easily, but he'd seen her need for a phone and filled it. And he'd done it in such a meaningful way. And then he'd listened to her last night when she'd expressed her regret over losing their text conversations and he'd printed it out.

Under that top page was a title page. The words were short and sweet.

Favorite Story

By: Anna and Jax

"Oh my gosh," she crooned, pulling out the huge manuscript from the box.

This was her favorite present ever. He'd gifted her endless highs when she needed an escape from the hard stuff. She could pull out any page from these hundreds and be instantly transported to the moment they were having that conversation and how she felt—which with Jax, was always happy. Or as happy as she could be at the time.

Out loud, she admitted softly, "Aww, I like him."

The vision of his glowing green eyes flashed across her memory, but she didn't care. Because inside of this giant of a man, this dangerous man, this Titan Bad Bear, he cared, and he was sweet. Maybe the outside world couldn't see that part of him, but she did.

And lucky her that he had shown her this hidden piece of himself.

EIGHT

Annalise sat on the floor surrounded by pages of *Favorite Story*. She'd been devouring their old conversations for the past half hour.

There was a soft knock at the door. Hopeful, she stood and jogged over the scuffed wooden floors to answer it. Jaxon stood on the ground, right near the first porch stair, his hand on the back of his neck, chin lowered, with a look of such uncertainty in his lightened eyes.

"The present," she started, struggling for the words that would do her gratefulness justice. "Jax, that was everything."

Must've been good enough because his lips curved up in a stunning smile. Just a flash before it faded and he said, "Can I come in," in that gruff voice that said Titan was still close to the surface.

"Just so you know, my dirty mind wants to turn that perverted."

"Can I come in your house, and in you?" he said with a bad-boy grin.

"You were always good at playing."

The smile faded, and he leaned against the railing, staring toward the other cabins. "You needed the play. I could tell."

"You could?" she asked.

"Yeah. You would have quieter days, but the second we started playing, you would perk up and be your abnormal, funny, perverted, weird, perfect little self again. I didn't mind playing. It made me feel better, too."

She gave him a naughty smile. "You may enter my mansion."

"God," he muttered and then chuckled as he made his way up the stairs.

She expected him to just walk on through, but his hand slipped to her waist, and he squared up to her, pinning her against the doorframe. With a quick glance toward Ben's cabin, Jaxon leaned down and sipped at her lips. It was so surprisingly gentle that she melted against him immediately.

She loved everything about this. The way his hand stayed relaxed on her waist, as though they'd kissed a thousand times, and the way he tasted, the way his lips moved against hers like gently rolling lake waves. The way both of their animals stayed silent, like they were giving their human sides a moment to just be together, no reminders that they were monsters.

It was the most normal moment she'd experienced since she'd been Turned.

And Jax was the one giving it to her.

Awww, I like him.

Her stomach fluttered as he switched the angle of his kiss and pressed himself against her firmly. No man had ever been able to draw this kind of reaction from her body. Every cell reached for him, like they could never be close enough.

He dipped his tongue past her lips, but didn't push for more. Instead, he rested his forehead against hers and let off a shaky sigh. Eyes closed, he brushed his fingertips down her arms and linked their hands. And then he said something that confused her.

"You're terrifying."

She squeezed his hands. "Jax, look at me."

He opened his eyes, and she immediately knew why he'd been hiding. The color there was such a light and unnatural green, they were almost painful to look at.

She frowned, dragged his hand to her lips, and pressed a kiss onto his knuckles. "You have nothing to be afraid of with me."

"You're wrong," he said low, shaking his head as he eased back and stood straight and tall again. "You're so wrong, Anna."

"She-Devil is not a threat to Titan."

He huffed a humorless laugh and let his fingers fall from hers, then strode inside the house. As she shut the door, he made his way through the small living room. He brushed his fingers against the back of the couch as he passed and then picked up the trinkets she'd placed on the mantle of the small fire place.

"Presents from Samuel, my brother," she explained as he held up the snow globe with the fish in the middle. "He travels, and he picks me up snow globes from the airports when he's away. He's done it since he was twenty-one. I don't know why, but now it's tradition. It's silly, but I love them."

"You're close to your brother?" he asked, as he made his way into the kitchen.

"Very close. We're only two years apart. He's the only one in my real life who knows about the panther. He built the cage I slept in, and shifted in." It hurt to think about the cage, so she did a hard right turn and changed the subject. "I heard you have a brother, too."

"Twin brother. We're close, but half the time I love him, and half the time our bears are brawling." He chuckled and had a faraway look in his eyes. "Our human sides have always gotten along. Our bears have not."

Annalise locked her arms against the back of the couch and grinned. "And you're a Gray Back," she said, testing what he would let her talk about. "You both were born little monsters, right?"

Jaxon ghosted her a quick grin. "You've been talking to the panthers about me, huh?"

"I got in trouble for not researching enough," she said cheerily. "I learn quick."

"Mmm," he hummed as he sat up on the counter

and jerked his chin in a come-hither gesture that made the butterflies in her stomach get to flapping again. Jaxon Barns was sexy, and he knew it.

As she approached and then settled between his legs, she rested her hands on his thighs. Jaxon brushed her hair off her shoulders. "The panthers don't understand the dynamics of other crews. That's because they keep to themselves. It's instinct for them. Maybe for She-Devil, too. But for me, growing up with the Gray Backs was normal. Violence was normal. We would cuss and brawl and bleed, and then we would have a beer and go about our lives until the next time we needed to fight."

"Needed to?"

"Yeah." He shrugged. "Fighting feels good, and relieves tension."

"And Gray Backs...they just get along after fights?"

"Sometimes. Sometimes one of us will be mad for a week, but we all got over it. We had to."

"Why?"

"Because we were crew. It'll be the same here. You won't always get along. It's not a perfect or easy life, Anna." He cocked a dark eyebrow. "It was sexy as fuck watching you go after Ben on my behalf yesterday. And when you turned on Barret? I get hard every time I think about it. You're a fierce little kitty."

"I thought you weren't into shifter girls."

Jaxon scratched under his chin, at the line of his dark beard, and narrowed his eyes. "Pass. I know you're wanting to know, but I'm here, aren't I?"

"Would you rather me be human?" she pushed.

"Yes," he said without hesitation.

It hurt. It was like the end of a whip against cold skin. It stole her breath. She wished she was human too, but hearing Jaxon assuredly say she wasn't right...well, it made her heart hurt in ways it hadn't before.

"Not because of me, Anna. I wish your life was easier. I can see your future here, and it's probably very different from what you're used to. But I can't be in it."

More hurt. More ache.

"What if Ben changes his mind and lets you in the crew?"

"I'm a rogue."

"So?"

He gathered her hair into little pigtails at the back

of her neck. "You don't understand. I'm nomadic. I didn't pledge to a crew. I can't. My bear doesn't want to settle. I wander. I can't stay in one place for more than a few days."

"But if you tried—"

"You think I haven't tried, Anna? I've warred with my bear my whole life. I hate what I am. I want a home. The most I can hope for is finding a girl who will be okay with roaming."

"Don't talk about other girls," she growled, fury whipping through her. "Don't sit here playing with my hair, looking me in the eyes, and talk about some future girl who is a better match. Fuck her. You said you're here. Well...so am I."

A low rumble emanated from his chest, and his eyes flashed with intensity. For an instant, she thought it was anger that had transformed his face into something wild, up until the point a slow, feral smile stretched his lips. "I like when you get possessive. It's sexy. Makes me want to spin you around and fuck you from behind." Her jerked his chin. "Right up against that counter over there."

The anger in her evaporated instantly and was replaced by the stunned, shaky feeling her body always got when he had texted to her like that. How many naughty discussions had they had in the last four months? How many times had his words left her legs trembling, and her stomach quivering with desperation to have him buried deep inside of her? And now he was here. Now those sexy words weren't in a text for her to read. She didn't have to imagine his voice. She could hear the deep timbre of it and see the desire in his eyes as he dragged his gaze down her body.

She could actually have him.

"Yes, please," she whispered.

The sexy smile fell from his lips and he slid off the counter, catching her hand on his thigh and placing it on the hard length of his erection pressing against his jeans.

Oh God, how could a man be this sexy?

He stalked her, pushing her by the hips backward until her ass hit the counter on the other side of the small kitchen. Such hunger roiled in his eyes. The second he leaned down and pressed his lips to hers, he slid his hand down the front of her shorts, cupped his hand on her sex and pushed a finger into her. She inhaled deeply at how surprising and good the sensation was. Jax was a man who knew exactly how to touch a woman. She was clay in his capable hands. Not submissive in the bedroom in general, but right now, she would've done anything he asked.

His free hand went to the side of her neck and held her in place as he deepened the kiss, plunging his tongue into her mouth. Annalise let off a tiny helpless whimper and unsnapped the button on his jeans. It sounded so loud in the quiet of the kitchen. She brushed her fingertips against the swollen head of his hard cock, and Jax reacted, thrusting against her with a soft, sexy groan. Desperate, she shoved his jeans down his hips, exposing the muscular V at his waist. Jax pulled his hand from her shorts, shrugged out of his blue flannel shirt, then reached over his head, and pulled off his black T-shirt, leaving his hair mussed as he tossed the fabric onto the floor. His massive shoulders rippled with muscle as he moved to grip her waist again. His fingers dug into her skin as his lips collided with hers again. The kiss was urgent now, the pace of his stroking tongue fast and hard as he pressed his hips against hers.

To touch his skin was a need. It wasn't a want. To exist another moment, she *needed* to feel the warmth of his skin against hers. Annalise eased back just enough to tug her shirt off, though much less graceful than Jax had. He helped. He peeled it from her arms the rest of the way in a rush, and then reached behind her and popped the clasp of her bra like he'd written the damn book on being a smooth operator. Hooking his finger in the front of her bra, he yanked it off her arms and, without hesitation, moved to her shorts. He didn't even unbutton them, just shoved them along with her panties down to her ankles so she could step out of them. He stepped back with the smack of his lips, cast a quick glance down at the pile of fabric, and grinned.

She'd worn pink see-through lacies today, just in case number one on her list did happen.

He slid a firm hand to her breast and massaged as he pressed his hard erection against her belly. So warm. Surely, Jax ran ten degrees hotter than her. She wanted to study all his tattoos and ask about every one of them. She wanted to know the story he'd had drawn on the canvas of his body, but that would have to wait because right now, she just wanted to close her eyes and feel him. And not just him, but the blanket of safety he laid over her every time he was physically close. It was broad daylight, and she wasn't insecure at all about her body. She'd never trusted anyone this much, and she'd only just met him in person.

Inside of her, She-Devil was quiet and watchful. Happy almost. Well, that was new.

Jax gripped her hips and spun her slowly while kissing her. When she faced the counter, right before he disengaged from the kiss, he sucked hard on her bottom lip, bit it slightly. Oh, she liked bitey. Or more specifically, She-Devil did.

Annalise's body was on fire, and the warmth gathered and pooled between her thighs. Anticipation built in her lower belly when Jax gripped the back of her hair and pushed her forward so that her bare breasts rested on the cool surface of the counter. She thought he would ease into her, but the second the head of his cock pushed into her wet entrance, Jax thrusted hard and stretched her in an instant. The growl was back in his throat now as he reared back and shoved into her again. So big, but she was ready and relaxed and this didn't hurt at all. It felt so fucking good, she was left breathless with every thrust. And then he reached around her hip and pressed his fingers on her clit, rubbed in rhythm to him slamming into her, and she cried out at how sensitive she was. Jax massaged her breast with the other hand, pinning her against the counter as he bucked into her, over and over, faster and harder until she was crying out with every stroke, so close to release.

When he leaned against her and bit down on her neck, the pressure in her middle built to blinding, and her orgasm was instant with the pressure of his teeth on her skin. She screamed his name as he pounded into her. The quick, deep pulses were so fast, and she was so responsive to their connection right now, it was almost a relief when he snarled and shoved deep inside her, froze as the first jet of warmth throbbed from his cock.

His teeth were still on her as he bucked into her again and again with the rhythm of his own pulsing release.

"Do it," she said mindlessly. Do what? He was giving it to her hard, had given her an orgasm that was stretching on and on. What was she asking?

Jax's jaws clenched so that he was close to piercing her skin. It hurt. What kind of violent creature in her middle would ask for this? What kind of monster would ask that a man she cared for hurt her?

Still she begged. "Please, Jax."

The bite got harder. He would draw blood with it. Warmth was streaming down her inner thighs, and they were still throbbing together, matching each other's orgasms, but suddenly, Jax released her neck and pulled out of her so fast, it was shocking.

Legs shaking and splayed, she leaned against the counter, panting, wondering where the all-consuming warmth had gone. In that instant of disconnect, she missed his touch down to her bones. Her instincts told her something was very wrong.

"Fuck," Jax choked out in a strange, gravelly voice. "Anna..."

Annalise turned just in time to see Jax fall to his knees, his body rippling with breaking bones.

"Anna, run!" he yelled.

She didn't understand. They'd just shared everything. They'd been connected and happy. They'd satisfied each other, so why was Titan shredding his skin right now? Annalise forced her legs to move and bolted for the door as the massive grizzly ripped out of Jax and bellowed a roar that shook the house. With a gasp, Annalise threw open the door. She could hear him coming, his nails scrabbling across the wooden floors, the cabin shaking with every step he gained on her.

Outside, there was movement on her right. The panthers were coming. She didn't know which ones, but three solid black monster cats were barreling toward her so fast they nearly blurred. There was panic in the first's eyes. Ben?

She leaped off the porch as Titan blasted through the front wall. Splinters and logs exploded outward. Her back stung, but she had no time to favor anything. She had to put distance between her and the grizzly. Her middle turned molten, and with no warning, She-Devil burst from her skin. She pitched forward and landed on all fours, then spun around. She-Devil wasn't a runner.

There was war. Awful war. The panthers and grizzly were all tearing each other to shreds. Red Havoc had come to protect her, but the beast they were defending her from was the beast she adored. Who did she hurt? Who did she side with? Who did she sink her claws and teeth into?

Confused, she sank to her belly in the mud and hissed, frantic gaze going back and forth between the panthers latched onto the bear. Green rage flashed in his eyes as he latched his massive jaws onto one of the panther's legs and ripped the cat off him. The panther slid off-balance through the mud and tried to struggle to its feet, but his back leg was clearly broken. He couldn't even put pressure on it, and it was stuck at an odd angle. The constant growl in his throat sounded pained. Was that Anson?

"Shit! Stop!" Jax's voice echoed across the clearing.

Stunned, Annalise looked over to find him completely human, on his knees in the grass, streaming red from a cut across his chest but otherwise looking in fine health.

He held his hands up to stop the two panthers stalking closer. "I'm in control! I'm in control again, but you'll bring the bear back if you don't stop!" Jax gripped his stomach and doubled over. He needed help. The panthers would kill him in his human form, or draw Titan out again and start the battle all over.

Annalise bolted for him and skidded to a stop between Ben and Jax. She flattened her ears against her head and hissed, then slapped a claw at Ben's face when he got too close. She didn't understand what was happening, but she couldn't watch them fight again and do nothing. She-Devil's instincts were too big, too wild, too much to stand aside and let this happen.

Fuck. Consequences.

Jax was hers, monster and all.

As Ben Changed back, he let off a panther scream that morphed into the word, "Fuuuuck!" His human face was red, his veins popping in his neck, his eyes bright gold and furious. He ran his hands through his blond hair and then gripped the top as he paced, eyes on Jax, who was still on his knees behind her.

"You were with her for fifteen fuckin' minutes, Grizzly! And you tried to kill her."

"Bite her," Jax corrected.

"What?" Ben yelled.

"I want to claim her."

"No!"

"I know!" Jax yelled, standing gracefully. "I told her to run. I stopped myself, but the bear pushed for the bite."

"Uh, guys?" Anson gritted out from where he was

lying like an upended turtle in the mud. "My leg hurts so bad." He rolled back and forth on his back, like that would ease the pain. The bruising and swelling was already getting bad. Indeed, it looked awful. Jax had snapped it in his jaws. They needed to call 911!

"Mother fucker cock chafer asshole licker bag of dicks Gray Back!" Anson yelled.

Barret was human now and snorted. Hands on his hips, eyes shining with hunger, he announced, "We should kill him."

"Kill me?" Anson screeched.

"No, you dumbass," Barret said. "The Gray Back. He gave us good reasons...right, Alpha?"

He swung his attention to Ben, who sighed. "Barret, we can't just kill everyone. It's not a solution for everything."

"I never get to have any fun!" Barret the Hillbilly Serial Killer yelled, and then he stomped off toward his cabin.

As Annalise forced herself to Change back, Jax made his way smoothly over to Anson.

"Don't touch my cat," Ben demanded, following him closely. "Attack him while he's on his back, and I will let Barret have you!"

"I'm not attacking him. I told you I'm in control right now. You keep calling me a Gray Back like it's a cuss word. Well, asshole, being raised in that crew is about to benefit this mother fucker bag of dicks Red Havoc panther. Quit squirming and man up," Jax muttered, feeling along Anson's leg.

"Don't touch me!" Anson kicked at Jax and screamed in agony when he connected.

"Big *and* dumb. Way to kill the panther stereotype, you pansy," Jax said. Was that amusement in his voice? What the hell was happening?

"Why are you smiling like that?" Anson said, curling his fists against his chest and shrinking back into the mud as he looked up at Jax suspiciously.

"Oh, I don't know." Jax gripped Anson's calf in both hands and twisted his shoulders sharply as he set the bone. *Snap!*

Anson screamed. And screamed.

Jax ignored it even though it must've hurt his ears to be that close to the sheer and monstrous volume of Anson's pained yell. "You all talk about Gray Backs like they're so different from you. False. You're the Gray Backs of the panthers. Fuckin' C-team." Jax pointed toward where Barret was kicking the side of his cabin over and over. "You have Murder Kitty…" He jammed a finger at Anson. "Pussy Panther." And where are your others, Alpha? Lynn could be a freaking figment of your imaginations for all I know, Jenny is standing on your front porch grinning like all this is funny—the bloodthirsty female—and where's Greyson? Oh wait, there he is, sitting in that tree watching the fight. Smiling. Like a psychopath. And Ben, don't tell me fighting like that didn't feel good. I feel fucking great after that." Jax pointed at all of them, his dark eyebrows arched up. "C-team."

"Screw you, we're A-team panthers," Anson muttered in a hoarse voice as he felt over his calf with searching fingertips. "And good for you, Psycho Bear. You get your kicks from breaking bones."

"I re-set it, didn't I? That skill? It's one all the Gray Backs have. You're welcome."

"How often do you break each other's bones?" Ben asked an octave too high. His face was still the shade of a cherry.

Jax shrugged his shoulders and didn't answer.

Anson rolled up to a sitting position. He was a butt-naked, muddy mess. "You didn't make up a rude name for Princess Panther."

As everyone's gaze drifted to Annalise, she slowly covered up her lady bits as best she could. "Hi," she said lamely.

"Stop calling her Princess Panther. She can go by Annalise. She's perfect. A-team. The rest of you like to throw your judgement around, but what just happened here?" Jax said, leveling her with brownish green eyes. "Reminded me of home." His nostrils flared slightly. "Except it smells like moonshine and cat piss, and you have cabins instead of trailers."

"Speaking of, you destroyed Annalise's house." Ben did a Vanna White gesture toward the cabin Jax had barreled through. The entire front half of it was destroyed. Even the small loveseat was hanging off the porch. "We aren't exactly rollin' in the money, asshole."

"I'll fix it."

"No, you won't. You're banned from my territory. I take my mission back. I'll handle it. You just tried to kill Annalise—"

"Claim her, not kill her.

"Doesn't fucking matter, Grizzly! I saw you going after her. Your bear is out of control, and you drew all our panthers out and into battle. Maybe that was fun for you, but it wasn't fun for us!"

Anson raised his hand. "It was a little fun before he broke my leg."

"Shut up, Anson!" Ben yelled.

Anson zipped his mouth and pretended to throw away the key. But the slight curve of his lips said he was amused. God, this crew was weird.

Annalise slowly picked up a shredded couch cushion that was sitting on the lawn beside her and put it in front of her naked body. "I vote he isn't banned."

"This ain't up for votes!" Ben said, exasperated. "This is my call. I'm alpha, and all of your safety is my responsibility. There's blood every time you come here," Ben said, his pissed-off glare on Jax now. "No more. This is your warning. Next time you come up here, I'm listening to Barret."

"Yes!" Barret hissed from near his cabin. "You should come back tomorrow, Grizzly!"

"Oh, my God," Ben groaned, running his fingers down his face and looking exhausted. "Just leave. Go back to Damon's Mountains. You aren't welcome here."

"You remember Beaston's call?" Jax jerked his

head toward Annalise once. "You're supposed to let her go."

"I don't understand," Annalise spoke up.

Ben shook his head for a long time, hands on his hips. The silence in the clearing was deafening. "Beaston has no place here, and neither do his visions. I could've done it if I hadn't seen the look of determination in your eyes when you were going after her. I can't let you take her. You aren't safe, Jax. She isn't safe with you. Surely, you can see that."

There was a moment of surprise on Jax face, and then something awful happened. Annalise could practically see the realization wash through him as he dragged his attention to her. His eyes muddied to the soft brown of his human side, and his expression held ghosts. He glanced down at the long claw mark on his chest, kept his chin tucked, blinked slowly, and then looked at her again. "Anna..."

"Don't." She shook her head and approached him slowly. "Don't go."

"You need a crew—"

"But I need you, too."

"No, Kitty. Ben's right. You aren't safe with me. What can I give you? I can't be intimate with you anymore because this will happen. You'll beg for the bite and eventually I'll give in. And it'll hurt, Anna. It won't be gentle, or romantic. If I allow the bond, you'll be stuck with…" He gestured to himself.

But to her, being stuck with Jax sounded like the best thing in the world. He stood there tall and strong in front of her. Steady. Powerful legs, eight-pack flexing with each breath, covered in tattoos just right. Beard perfectly trimmed, eyes soft and sad, black hair mussed from the battle. Towering over her. Strong.

"I still feel safe," she whispered, her eyes burning. "I don't want you to go."

"It ain't his choice," Ben said.

Jax cast the alpha an angry glance and then stepped closer to Annalise. He pulled the cushion from her, tossed it into the mud, then gripped her shoulders gently. "Your place is here. I can see it clear as day. You'll get stronger here. You'll become as fierce as She-Devil up in these mountains. You need steady, Anna." Jax shook his head sadly. "I *wish*…more than anything…that I could be that for you. But I was born with Titan. I can't wreck your crew. I can't wreck your life. And I will if I stay."

A traitor tear escaped her eye. She wanted to be

strong because everyone was staring at her, and witnessing her heart being ripped out of her chest cavity. Jax was doing that, and he would hold it in his hand and drive away with it. And she would be left here, pretending for always that she was whole while an important part of her would be roaming the world with a rogue.

She closed her eyes tightly as he pulled her in close, and she slipped her arms around his back. This would be the last time she got to touch his skin. She-Devil was purring. Stupid cat. She didn't understand what this hug was.

It was goodbye.

"Jax—"

"Don't," he drawled, easing away from the hug. He stepped backward step-by-step. "Don't make this harder, or the bear will come back." Already his eyes were back to that painfully bright green, and he smelled like fur.

"I like you, Anna," he said, but she knew what he really meant. They'd said that to each other in all those messages because it had been too scary to say the L-word.

And she meant it when she forced the whispered

response past her tightened vocal chords. "I like you, too."

Jax turned and strode toward his truck.

Annalise's face crumpled, and she cried. What was the point of hiding her agony? She'd had him for a blinding moment of happiness, and now she had to go back to the loneliness because he was really leaving her.

Right before he disappeared into the Red Havoc woods, he gave her a quick glance out his open window. Such agony was etched into his expression Annalise's knees buckled, and she sank down into the mud, shoulders shaking with her sobbing.

"I'm sorry," Ben growled, and then he spun and made his way toward his cabin.

One by one, the panthers slunk into their homes until it was only her left, knees in the mud, her heart in the hand of the man she loved.

Annalise had come here so that life could be easier, but it had just gotten ten times harder.

Inside of her, She-Devil screamed her heartbreak.

NINE

One week.

One week, and Jax hadn't been able to force himself from Covington, the small town nestled in the Appalachian Mountains that was fifteen miles from *her*...from Annalise. His Anna. His She-Devil.

Something bad was happening to him.

He'd become stuck in this small town, as if his veins were full of slow drying cement, and he'd hardened day after day until he couldn't move at all. This was purgatory. Torture. He was so close to her, but so far away.

Every day was the same. He would wake up in the queen-size bed in the cheap motel and try to convince himself that today was the day he would really leave. Leave the Appalachian Mountains, leave Covington, leave the girl he'd left his heart with.

And just like every other day, he'd spent today trying to gather the courage to pack up his truck and drive back toward Damon's Mountains. Yet here he sat, in the dark of night, still in the hotel, still unable to leave.

But tomorrow would be the day. He'd made up his mind already and had worked himself up as he'd made his way through today. At the laundromat, he'd thought about her relentlessly. Thought about how he was taking care of her by leaving. At the diner where he'd eaten three burgers and two orders of fries, he'd thought about pounding her from behind against the counter in her house. The house Titan had destroyed. He'd convinced himself that was just the beginning if he stayed in her life. He was a destroyer.

If she'd been human...if only she'd been human. That's what he'd been searching for, so he could avoid this bond he already felt tugging at him so hard. He had wanted a mate, but not love. Not devotion like this. He hadn't wanted to tether Titan to anyone.

He hated the bear. Hated being a shifter. Always had, and always would, because Titan stunted his life.

He cut his hope for happiness off at the knees and forced himself to keep his expectations low so that he wouldn't be disappointed in life. Hope was a slippery slope for a man like him. Wishing for a bigger life than he was capable of would make his animal unmanageable.

Dressed in briefs and nothing more, he sat on the edge of his bed, elbows on his knees, face in his hands. He'd stopped looking in the mirror at himself. His face was too haunted, and it was all because of this decision.

Stay or go? Stay or go? Stay or go?

Where was his fucking urge to roam when he needed it?

His phone rang. Terror, hope, desperation, and urgency had him reaching for it in a rush. Maybe it was Annalise again.

It hurt to read her messages. He could hear the heartache in her words, but he was trying to be a good mate. A good mate? Fuck. He should've never come after her. He'd ruined them both with that decision.

The number on the caller ID wasn't the phone he'd bought her, though. He'd been good and not responded to her texts. But this wasn't her.

"Hello?" he asked gruffly after he connected the call.

"Grizzly."

Fucking Ben.

"What do you want?" he asked, pissed to hear the alpha's voice right now.

"A favor."

Jax snorted. "I don't owe you anything."

"Are you still hunting Brody?"

"Maybe. If I am, it's not for you. It's for her."

"Well, this favor is for her, too. And surely you know how hard it is for me to ask. You're still in Covington. I've been watching you. Waiting for you to leave. You can't, can you?"

"None of your goddamn business."

When Ben sighed, static blasted across the phone. "I need you to come see something. Something I don't know how to deal with. Something I need help with. It's about Annalise."

"When?" Jax asked, panic flaring through his chest. What if she was hurt? Or what if she'd run away?

"Now. Right now. Speed." The line went dead.

"Shhhit," Jax muttered as he stood and reached for his clothes on the back of the hotel room chair. Ben was an alpha just like Creed of the Gray Backs. He wouldn't ask for help until something really bad happened.

The keys scratched the table as he grabbed them too hard, but screw it. Before he even had his jeans zipped, boots tied, or his shirt settled over his stomach, he was out the door and jogging toward his truck.

Please no cops. He couldn't get pulled over right now as he blasted up the mountain road that lead to Red Havoc territory. His mind was racing with what could be wrong. Maybe Annalise was hurt, or sick. Nah, not sick. Shifters didn't get sick like humans. There was a bright side to She-Devil he hadn't thought about before. Okay, not sick. Maybe was lost in the woods? Why was this trip up into the mountains taking so long?

The truck nearly went up on two wheels when he turned right onto the worn, one-lane dirt road. He blasted past the old, dilapidated wooden fence with the No Trespassing signs and Turn Back Now signs that had been riddled with holes, probably from a shotgun peppering them.

When at last he skidded to a stop in the clearing in front of the Red Havoc cabins. He scanned it frantically to find a single panther shifter. Greyson. He was leaned against the ruined porch of Annalise's cabin, eyes haunted. Inside of Jax, Titan was riled up, ready to steal his skin. Every instinct he possessed was blaring. Something was so wrong.

He threw the truck into park and cut the engine, then got out and bolted for Greyson. "Where is she?"

"This way," the quiet man said solemnly, jerking his chin toward the mountains behind Annalise's destroyed cabin.

When Greyson took off at a jog, Jax followed, zipping his pants as he went. No time to tie his shoes, he kicked out of them completely. He was used to running around Damon's Mountains barefoot.

A panther screamed in the dark, and the sound drew chills from his skin. Jax slowed slightly. That was She-Devil, but he didn't recognize the call. He couldn't tell if she was hurt or angry. He ran faster behind Greyson, who had kicked up the pace the second another scream followed.

Up and up the mountain they ran until they

reached the broken-down fence and the deer trail. It even smelled like Annalise. What the hell was she doing up here?

Greyson dropped in front of him and morphed into his panther like there was no pain at all. His cat took off at a sprint, and Jax pushed his legs harder to keep up. At a clearing, Ben stepped out in front of him on the trail. Jax skidded to a stop on the dirt path to avoid slamming into him as Greyson ran to join a cat fight.

She-Devil was at the middle of it, brawling. Slapping, hissing, ears flat, eyes like gold fire. The crew ducked in and out, taking slaps, herding her back toward Jax.

"What the fuck are they doing?" Jax lurched forward to Change and defend her, but Ben slapped a hand on his chest and pushed him back with a strength that surprised him.

"Look," he said, tilting his head toward the edge of his territory, up where Jax had asked Annalise to meet him last week. Where his truck had been were four sets of glowing eyes. In the dark, four massive male lions paced the property line.

"She's calling them in," Ben said low.

"I don't understand."

Ben sighed and crossed his arms over his chest, stared at his crew as they attacked She-Devil again. "They're trying not to hurt her, but she can't cross that territory line or the pride will take her."

"Take her?"

"She's in heat. Went into it right after you left last week. Did you know she sleepwalks?"

"No," Jax said, stunned.

"Her cat...she's broke as fuck. The name She-Devil suits her. Since the day she came to me, she's been shifting in her sleep. I'm guessing that's why she had herself locked in that cage room at nights, to protect the outside world from She-Devil. As far as we can tell, Annalise isn't there at nights, Jax. She's just a wild panther, running on instinct.

She-Devil screamed again, and something about the agony called to Titan.

"At first, we took shifts. We each took turns Changing with her and keeping her in the territory, keeping her safe. I thought if She-Devil claimed the territory and learned the boundaries, she would settle, and we could eventually stop shifting with her at nights. Maybe even trust her eventually. But there's a bachelor pride of lions way too damn close to our territory, and after you left, She-Devil started taking her body any time. Not just when she was sleeping. She's shifting four or five times a day right now. You leaving didn't do what I had hoped it would. It broke something inside of her cat."

"What do mean?" Jax asked, troubled down to his bones as he watched his mate fight with her own crew.

Ben signed and arched his gaze to Jaxon. "She's calling for you."

Jax squatted down and watched her brawl in the dark. Dominant badass she-panther, she was fully engaged with the biggest one, Barret, right now, and not backing down an inch.

"Jax...what you're watching right now? She's taking Second."

"Oh, my God," he murmured, standing and linking his hands behind his head. Ma was the only female holding Second in a crew right now, and what had he done? He'd gone and found himself a she-shifter as dominant and badass as her. But unlike with Ma, She-Devil wasn't a stable member of the crew. A high rank for an uncontrolled animal would cripple Red Havoc.

"Why did you bring me here to watch this?" Jax asked.

"You know why."

Jax lost it and shoved him backward against a tree. He pulled the alpha by the shirt and slammed him back against it a second time for good measure. He knew why this fuckface was letting him witness his mate taking Second. "You gonna put her down, Ben? You gonna kill her?"

"For the good of my crew."

"Fuck you. I'll rip you from throat to dick and make you watch me piss on your intestines before I'd allow it. Call your panthers off her, or your mate will be a widow tonight."

Ben looked sick, but shook his head. "We've been at this for days, Jax. We're exhausted. There's no sleep happening. She will bring the lions on top of us. She will deplete us, and when she's sitting on that throne as Second, with power over the boys, she's gonna to wreck us from the inside out. No one will be salvageable."

Jax was gonna kill him. He was going to snap his neck, and then he was going to Change and murder the panthers at war with his mate. And then after he roared his victory over their carcasses, he was going after the lions. He didn't give a single fuck if he died for this. He couldn't let her be put down. She was his to protect.

"You came from a crew under Creed Barnett," Ben said low.

The sound of the panther fight and the roar of a lion pacing the territory line made Jax dizzy. *Kill them all.*

The question confused him. With a frown, he asked, "So?"

"So, I always respected him for taking in the broken shifters. That's what I've done. I know how hard it must've been for him because it's agony for me."

"Spit it out, Panther."

"I need help, or I can't save this one."

Chest heaving, Jax pushed off Ben and took a few steps back. He paced the trail, eyes on the panther fight. The biggest panther was slinking away, totally mauled with claw and tooth marks. She-Devil had no blood matting her fur. She screamed again, and it sounded triumphant.

Annalise had just taken Second. Shit.

What was he supposed to do? How could he help her?

In his pocket, Jax's phone rang.

The name on the caller ID drew gooseflesh on his entire body.

Beaston.

Jax brought the phone slowly up to his ear, eyes on his mate as she went to war with the other two panthers.

"Jax, bring her to me," Beaston said in that low, gravelly, feral voice of his. "Bring her home."

TEN

Aching muscles woke Annalise. When she cracked her sleepy eyes open, only dark gray light filled the room. She hadn't been sleeping well, and every cell in her body was on fire. She-Devil was killing her.

The scent of Jax's cologne and fur brushed her senses, and she struggled up onto locked arms in her bed.

He sat in the corner, no chair, just sat with his back against the wall, his knees bent, elbows resting on them, hands linked behind his head, black hair mussed and looking like he hadn't slept in days. He was the most beautiful thing she'd ever laid eyes on.

"Tell me you're real," she murmured. "Tell me you brought my heart back."

Without a word, Jax stood up to his full height and sauntered over to her, then slipped under the covers behind her and pulled her against his chest. His lips stayed gentle on the back of her neck, and then he did something beastly and perfect. He sank his teeth into her skin there so hard and fast, she had no time to flinch.

As quickly as he'd bitten her, he released her torn flesh and licked the warmth that trailed down her back. Over and over he ran his tongue until the pain eased and the bleeding stopped.

My monster. Mine.

Feeling raw and broken and so ashamed she'd let him claim her before she explained how doomed she was, she turned over in his arms and snuggled as close as possible to him, just to selfishly absorb the feeling of safety he gave her before she admitted something that would make him run.

He wrapped his arms tight around her back. So warm and strong, his pecs were hard against her cheek.

"Everything is going to be okay," he murmured in the darkness before dawn.

That was the most beautiful combination of six

words in the English language, but for someone like her, they couldn't ever be true. "It's not," she said. "I hurt people. I can't stop hurting people. I don't have any control of the cat. I never did."

"It's okay. I'm going to take care of you."

And because she needed to purge her soul to the man she trusted more than anyone, she told him her deepest, darkest secret. "A man named Brody asked me on a date. And afterward, he kissed me at my door like a gentleman. And when I said goodnight and tried to shut the door on him, he forced his way in, took me to my bedroom, and hurt me."

Against her, Jax went rigid, but stayed silent.

"And while he was hurting me, he bit me. She-Devil came out immediately."

"He'll die for what he did," Jax murmured. "I'm already hunting him."

Her face crumpled, and she buried her face against him to hide her weak tears. "You don't have to. She-Devil killed him."

There was a beat of stunned silence, and then Jax soothed her with a, "Shhhhh. Beautiful, brawling, courageous, badass Second of the Red Havoc Crew, it wasn't murder. It was justice. She-Devil followed the rules of our people. She did good."

"She was born of violence, and her first act was awful, Jax. And now I can feel the good parts of me shrinking to nothing. I know what's coming. I see what she does at night, and in the daytime, too. I'm there, in the smallest corner of her messed up mind. I can see what she does, and I can't stop her. I want you so bad, but I'm worse than ever now. Ben will put me down soon. He has to. And sometimes, when I'm exhausted and my body hurts like hell from the constant Changing, I think I'll be relieved when he does."

"Don't talk like that. You're on a journey, Anna. You've got yourself through the hard part. You're tired and you're limping. But you aren't doing this alone anymore. I'm here. I'll carry you until you can stand on your own two feet again. That bite mark on your neck? That wasn't Titan's pledge to She-Devil. That's me, Jaxon Barns, telling you I'm fucking *in* this with you. I'll carry you on my goddamn back until you can walk on your own again. But I *will not* allow you to be put down. You aren't done with this life yet, little badass. You just got a big old beast put inside you, and you have to learn how to work with her."

"How?"

"With support. You have Samuel and Red Havoc. And first and foremost, you have me for as long as you want. For every breath, every smile, every tear, I'll be here right here beside you. Leaving didn't fix anything for either of us. It hurt She-Devil, it hurt you, it hurt me, it hurt Titan. I tried to let you go so you could have a better life, but it didn't take. So, this is where we dig our toes in against the hurricane that is your monster kitty and walk through the damn storm together. Deal? No quitting. I won't let you."

It felt so damn good to hear him pledge to weather her storm. *So* damn good. "I've done this alone this whole time," she whispered. "It was awful. I had to let go of all my friends and family except for Samuel. If I hadn't had you all those months, texting me, making me laugh and feel normal for precious minutes at a time, I would've buckled under She-Devil. You've been propping me up this whole time, and when you left last week, I fell."

"I won't let you fall again, Anna," Jax promised, cupping her cheeks. He pressed a kiss to the top of her head. "I swear to you I'll keep you propped up until you get your strength back. Even if I have to stay

awake every night to keep She-Devil safe, I'll do it."
He swallowed hard and lowered his voice. "I couldn't
ever figure out why I was given Titan. I used to be so
angry about him. Just...pissed off at whatever power
decided that I needed to be the one to manage him.
But last night, I was watching you fight your crew,
watching how tough you are, and this thought filled
my head. Maybe I'm Titan because you need me to be.
You aren't alone anymore. You never will be again."
His hands gentle on her cheeks, he eased her back
and dipped his lips to hers. He drank her in slowly,
his lips moving smoothly against hers. Slowly, he
disengaged from the kiss and arched his back, drew
her lips to the place right over his heart. "Your turn,
Anna."

"You want my bite? Even after what I told you?"

Jaxon's smile was slow and evicted the sadness
from his expression. "Now I know we match, Kitty. I
didn't want to be the only monster between us,
dragging you down for always."

"Now you know I'm a monster, too."

"A hot monster." His white teeth flashed. "A hot
monster who needs to stop calling those damn lions
into the territory or I'm gonna have to get all

murdery. If you want dick, I'm your man."

Annalise snorted a surprised laugh. "Didn't you know those calls weren't for the lions? She-Devil has been trying to get back to the place we were first together. She's been hunting for you. She didn't understand why you left."

"Well," he murmured, voice going low and soft. "Make it to where I can never leave again."

Annalise searched his eyes, but there was nothing but sincerity in the soft brown color there. Inhaling deeply, she smiled up at him and said, "I like you." She waited for his answering smile before she sank her teeth into his pec, right over his heart. He held her head closer, encouraging her, and didn't flinch or gasp at the pain. That was for her. He was making it easier for her to hurt him. Good mate.

She pulled away and wiped the iron-tasting warmth from her lips with the back of her hand. "Now I'm truly a monster," she whispered.

Jax shook his head slowly and looked down at her with the proudest expression on his face. He ran a light touch over the painful bite on her neck. "No, Anna. Now you're claimed. Get on up, grab a few pair of those sexy granny panties, and pack a bag."

"Why?"

"Because Ben has released you to me until I can get you stronger."

Annalise frowned in confusion and drew back, searched his face in the early morning light. "How will you do that?"

"With help."

"From who?"

Jaxon's smile stretched his face. "From the Gray Backs."

ELEVEN

Annalise wrung her hands nervously. A day and a half drive had turned into two and a half days thanks to She-Devil taking her body twice in Jaxon's truck. She rested her head back against the shredded headrest and felt like a jerk. His truck had been really nice before she'd sharpened her claws on it.

He'd done well both times to pull over to the side of the road and drag her out before she could destroy it completely, but he was sporting a few new scars now thanks to the black-furred hellion living inside of her. A juicy bug splatted against the windshield, and she snarled. Already her skin was tingling as if she would Change again.

"Can we revisit the idea of a cage room?" she

asked Jax.

"You won't need one up here. You won't hurt anyone. If you fight them, they'll just enjoy the bloodbath. Change all you want. You aren't dangerous to the shifters in Damon's Mountains."

"So, explain again why I have to be the Second of Red Havoc?"

"Because you kicked Barret's ass repeatedly. That last one he took as a challenge and really went at you, and you took your claws to him and demoted Murder Kitty to Third."

Annalise giggled. "Murder Kitty should be my name."

Jax made a ticking sound behind his teeth, barely audible over the sound of the country song on the radio. The Beck brothers were playing. She loved them.

"Brody wasn't murder," Jax said. "He was revenge. Any man who hurts a woman like that deserves worse than you gave him. He's lucky. I would've done it slow." Jax's voice lowered and became too rough to be human. "I would've made it last a couple of days. Maybe given him to the Gray Backs when I was bored. Maybe let Damon light him up and devour his ashes. Trust me, Anna, you did Brody a favor he didn't deserve. You'll get no judgement from me or anyone else for She-Devil defending you like that."

"I know who Damon is. I've been researching," she said, holding up her phone and shaking it slightly. The sunlight caught the jewels on the skull case.

"Thata girl, and what did you learn?"

"Damon Daye, aka the blue dragon, reigns over these mountains. There are three crews. The Ashe Crew, the Boarlanders, and your Gray Backs. And most of them make a living by being lumberjacks. Ha. Are you a Lumberjack Werebear, Jax?"

He chuckled, slid his free hand over her thigh, and squeezed gently. Warmth immediately dumped into her center just from his easy and comfortable touch. He'd seen her at her worst over the last two days of traveling and trying to control She-Devil, and he was still here. Still laughing and touching her. Still supporting her.

He wore a blue baseball cap on backward today. He was scruffy-sexy with his unshaven face, dark eyes, white T-shirt, and jeans with holes at the knees. And he sat here with her, the epitome of a relaxed man, steering wheel turning in one hand, and an easy smile on his lips, like she wasn't going to shift at any moment. He wasn't scared of her at all.

Good man. Strong man. Her man.

"I did work logging jobs some of the seasons, but mostly I'm a worm farmer." He slid her a huge grin. "Does that turn you on?"

"A worm farmer?" she asked, waiting for the punchline.

"It's a family business. My ma built this worm empire from the ground up, and now her worms are the biggest name in bait worms and compost worms in the world. Willa's Worms."

"Oh, my gosh, I've seen those in the store! In the hunting and fishing section. They are stored in those little refrigerators by the cash register. The logo is pink and blue and has a cartoon worm. I always thought it was so cute."

"Yep. I take care of shipping. They were there because I made it happen."

"So you aren't really a farmer then. You are on the business side."

"Oh, no. Ma wanted me and my brother to learn the business from the bottom up. I had to work my way into shipping. I started out with my hands dirty."

"And wormy," she teased. "So sexy. Jaxon Barns, professional worm wrangler. I'm so turned on right now." She wrapped her arms around her middle and snickered then tried to make a serious face and whispered, "Jax. I like your worm."

"Stop it."

"Maybe sometime, you wanna…stick it in my slimy wormhole."

"God, seriously? You sound like Ma right now. My worm is getting limp."

"Let me feel." She reached across his lap and petted his crotch.

"Hands off my worm."

"Heeeere, wormy, wormy, wormy."

"Woman, seriously, you're giving wormy a boner, cut it out. We're almost there. Or don't cut it out, but I'm gonna fuck you so hard against one of these trees, you'll be screaming my name and get us busted."

Holy hotness. "I wanna do that," she rushed out. "I wanna scream your name."

Jax slammed on the brakes, and the truck skidded sideways. He threw it into park the second it rocked to a stop and reached for her. "Take your pants off," he demanded.

Okay then. Bossy Jax was sexy.

She stripped out of her shorts faster than a lady of the night named Cinnamon, and then she crawled across the console and straddled Jax's lap. He already had his pants undone and shoved down his hips so his erection jutted up from between his powerful thighs. Hell yes to all of this—her body was already molten.

Jax gripped his cock as she lifted up and slid onto him, and together they let off twin groans of ecstasy as she lowered down slowly and took all of him. He gripped her hips so hard, it would've been uncomfortable if she was human, but She-Devil let off a snarl of appreciation.

"I fucking love when your eyes go gold like this," Jaxon gritted out. He leaned forward and plucked at the claiming mark on her neck with teasing, biting kisses. "Sexy." Bite. "Terrifying." Bite. "Badass." Bite. "Panther."

The pressure in her middle was already building in intensity as she bucked against him, her hips crashing with Jax's as he met her movement, stroke for stroke. They were already going too hard and too fast. This wouldn't last long, but he didn't seem to care. He pulled her down even harder on his dick, over and over until she was right on the verge, head thrown back, eyes closed to the world, yelling out his name. Orgasm exploded through her as he drove deep and shot warmth into her in throbbing spurts. Her mind was gone. There was no worry in this moment. There was only the bone-deep sensation of belonging.

He'd called her a sexy, terrifying, badass panther and told her he loved the gold in her eyes. It was a far cry from when he'd admitted he wished she was human, and it meant the world to her that he accepted her now.

They slowed their pace and dragged out each other's aftershocks until they were twitching with sensitivity. And then she slid her hands up his chest and around his neck and nuzzled her cheek against his. She'd never done that with a man, but it felt right. It felt like saying I love you without the words, and she truly did. Something hummed between them, some electricity that hadn't been there before.

"Can you feel it?" he asked as he rubbed his cheek against hers. "Can you feel our bond?"

"Yes," she said, suddenly stunned. She eased back and looked down at their chests where it felt like a rope had been tied from his heart to hers, but there was nothing there. If he hadn't pointed it out, she would've thought herself even crazier. She would've thought it was She-Devil messing with her mind again.

"I never wanted a bond until you," Jax said, blazing green eyes locked on hers. "I wanted a half-life. I wanted an easy mate who wouldn't call to my bear. Who wouldn't make me wish for a better life."

"And now?"

"And now you're all I want. And if wishing for a better life means I can make you happy, keep you safe, and stable...well then, that's what I want. I like you just the way you are, Anna."

Her lip trembled, so she bit it to hide her emotions. "She-Devil and all?"

Jax leaned into her and angled his face, kissed her lips gently. And when he disengaged, she could see the utter honesty in his eyes when he murmured, "She-Devil and all."

TWELVE

Jaxon coasted through the piney Wyoming woods. Usually this last straightaway through Damon's Mountains made his stomach clench. The roamer in him would buckle about staying in his trailer and wouldn't want to settle into a few days of working here. The restlessness would be there, urging him to move on, even though he hadn't even seen the place yet.

It had always been like that. Since he was a cub, Titan wanted to move constantly.

Today was different, though. Today he had *her* with him.

Jax cast Annalise a sideways glance, just to see her reaction to the Grayland Mobile Park when she saw it for the first time. She was leaned forward, unbuckled already, sitting on the edge of her seat, bright gold eyes on the white gravel road, hands clenched on top of her thighs. She was humming with tension. She-Devil would come out again soon.

It made him happy and sad all at once. He was bonding with the animal side of her, too, and so damn glad now that she was a shifter and could handle this complicated life beside him. But Annalise was sore from all the quick Changes, and She-Devil was more unstable than ever. The shredded seats were proof of that.

At the low growl that rattled her throat, he dragged his attention back to the trailer park.

In front of the fire pit at the end of the road stood a man who was a sight for sore eyes. Blond hair, blue eyes, muscled up and wearing a white T-shirt like Jax's over holey jeans, also like Jax's. Clinton was about to give him so much shit for stealing his style.

Already, his eyes were narrowed and his arms were crossed over his chest. Fuckin' grumpy, half-psychotic Boarlander.

Jax parked by the fire pit and scanned the half circle of trailers behind it. There was another cluster of trailers off to the right, but no one seemed to be home. Usually this place was chaos.

Jax got out. "What the hell are you doing here, old man," he joked. Clinton always bristled at that. Shifters aged well. He looked thirty-five, forty, tops.

"The fuck you wearin', boy?"

"I wanted to match," Jaxon said, waiting at the front of the truck for Annalise to join him. She was walking too gracefully for how much her body was hurting. Yep, She-Devil was a-comin'. She slid her hand into his and waved at Clinton, who narrowed his eyes to bright blue little slits. His nostrils flared as he scented the air.

"Pussy," he said.

Annalise bristled beside Jax.

Clinton grinned remorselessly and finished, "Cat."

Jaxon glanced around suspiciously. "Seriously, what are you doing here? And where is everyone?"

"Gray Back Assholes are up at Bear Trap Falls. I'm here beautifying the place in their absence."

Jaxon threw a quick glance at Clinton's truck. The tailgate of his white Raptor was lowered, and in the bed were about twenty bags of fragrant fertilizer. "Whyyy?"

Clinton arched his blond brows. "Because last week Creed made a bet that I couldn't kick his ass in flip-cup, but I did. And then when he was supposed to pay up, he didn't."

"What was the bet?"

"He had to dress in one of Gia's tightest and prettiest dresses, a bright fuckin' red one, and wear lipstick and high heels and take a picture for me and Jason to post on our pages, but he pussied out." He gave Annalise a devil-may-care smile. "Not a cat joke. Creed really is a giant, gaping pussy."

Annalise giggled.

"So then I said I was gonna shit in his front yard if he didn't pay up," Clinton continued. "And I was going to, but my mate said I need to have better manners and it wasn't sanitary, blah blah blah, so this is the compromise. Happy wife, happy life. Wait, I can do better. Happy mate, and I don't have to masturbate."

Jaxon eyed the mowed yard in front of Creed and Gia's perfectly kept trailer. "You're gonna spread all that manure over Creed's yard?"

"Yeah. I got the smelly cow kind, too. You wanna help?"

Jax rubbed his jaw to hide his smile. "I would love

to, but I have to introduce my lady to the crew."

"Your lady? You mated, Jax?" Clinton asked.

Jax pulled his snarling little she-hellion against his side proudly. "Sure am. This is Annalise."

"Mmm," Clinton said, lifting his chin and glaring down his nose at Annalise. "You're broke as fuck, aren't you, pussy cat? You smell sick, sick, sick. It's okay. I'm sick, too. So are all the Gray Backs you're about to meet. Eternal fuck-ups, all of them."

Annalise pursed her lips into an upset little moue, and she smelled upset. She opened her mouth to say something, but Clinton bent smoothly and plucked a yellow weed flower out of the grass, then handed it to her. "Welcome to the C-team."

Looking utterly baffled, Annalise took the dandelion flower slowly from his hand.

Clinton spun on his heel with a flourish and flipped them off over his shoulder as he announced, "I've got shit to do."

Jaxon chuckled and pulled Annalise by the hand toward the trail in the woods that would lead to Bear Trap Falls.

"Should we…" she asked, her focus behind them where Clinton was unloading bags of fertilizer.

"Should we stop him?"

"Nah, Creed has it coming." He tossed her a grin over his shoulder. "A bet's a bet, and he didn't pay up."

THIRTEEN

Annalise couldn't keep her eyes from the big muscle-man currently ripping into a giant bag of lawn poop. He swiveled his leg and punted an old pink flamingo that had been stabbed into the yard in front of one of the trailers, and it went sailing through the air and landed in the fire pit. Was he singing the "Beans, Beans, the Musical Fruit" song?

Jax's hand was relaxed in hers, but when she tripped over a gnarled tree root and pitched forward, he tightened his grip and supported her.

"Ow," she muttered, favoring her stubbed toe.

Her pink flip-flops clacked with every step and echoed through the lush, green woods. The trees here were tall with thick trunks and rough bark. The air smelled like pine sap and rich earth. And animals. Lots of different animals.

She-Devil snarled inside of her, and pain blasted through Annalise's stomach as she fought the urge to Change.

"It's okay if it happens here," Jax said fast. "You're safe."

Annalise swallowed over and over, trying to keep from retching. Her body hurt so bad. Her legs were stiff, her muscles felt torn to hell, and her joints ached with every movement. She-Devil would give her a slow death like Jax had promised Brody. It was ironic that she would go in the worst way out of the two of them, and she hadn't done anything wrong other than go on a date with an evil man. Well, and kill him after. Maybe this was Karma speaking.

As the animal scents grew stronger, another wave of pain took her, and she had to stop. "Jax, I'm sorry."

She could hear his sharp inhale before he turned around and canted his head, arched his dark eyebrow up and leveled her with those serious caramel brown eyes of his. "What did I say about saying sorry for things that aren't your fault? This ain't your fault."

She smiled from where she was bent over, head

thrown back so she could look up at him. She couldn't help herself.

"What's funny?"

"You said ain't."

With a deep, reverberating chuckle, he pulled her up straight again and hugged her to his chest. "I'll probably say it a lot. That's how people talk here."

"Well, then I ain't sorry for being about to Change uncontrollably and maul everyone."

Jax snorted and shook his head. "Woman, you can't hurt anybody here. I keep telling you. They'd welcome the fight. She-Devil can't scare any of the shifters in these mountains. It's not like with Red Havoc. You can't topple a crew here. Damon's Mountains are fuckin' concrete at this point. Been through more battles together than anyone would ever believe. You can do your worst, and they'll just laugh and play swat-the-kitty. Now, I won't let them hurt you too bad, but She-Devil's about to learn some tough lessons on proper animal behavior."

"So that's why we're here? To tame She-Devil?"

"No, Anna," Jax murmured, tone going deadly serious. "We're here to save you."

Right. Annalise forced her lips into a tight smile

and then followed him as he led her down the trail again. Poor Jax, thinking she could be saved. He didn't know She-Devil's thoughts, though. He wasn't in her head, listening to all the ways she planned on killing things around her. He hadn't heard She-Devil's plan to kill the Red Havoc Crew, and then move on to the lions just to sate her thirst for violence.

Thank God she hadn't been Turned into a dragon because she would've burned the world to ashes by now.

Every step was agony as her cells begged to morph into the panther. Chest heaving, she stepped out of the edge of the woods with Jax and winced against the harsh sunlight that shone from between two mountains in the distance. A sudden and piercing headache blasted across the back of her eyes.

The chatter of a crowd made her dizzy, and she swayed on her feet as she scanned the river in front of her.

"Anna," Jax said. "This is Bear Trap Falls."

There was indeed a waterfall that a tall man with black hair and dark eyes was diving from. It was one of those graceful ones that belonged to an Olympic diver. She'd only ever been good at belly flops.

"That's Creed," Jax said, gesturing to the man who hit the water with barely a splash. "He was my alpha growing up before I went rogue."

Further down the sandy beach, there were a couple dozen lawn chairs in neon pinks, oranges, greens, and blues. Tiki torches had been stuck in the ground, and there was a literal giant pulling a pair of beer bottles from an old, scuffed, blue cooler. Sitting in the chairs, there were at lease fifteen people talking and laughing. Some wore bathing suits, some wore cut-off shorts and flipflops like Annalise. The men wore mostly jeans with the rippling muscles of their chest and abs on full display. The pervert in her rejoiced. Across the river a few shirtless men were tossing a football and having a loud, echoing argument about who threw the most like a girl.

In the sky, a falcon circled, and through the woods she could see movement. A massive silverback gorilla walked beside a chestnut-colored grizzly bear, both sets of eyes warily on her as they made their way slowly through the trees.

Beside her, Jax lurched forward as someone shoved him from behind, and Annalise reacted. She snarled and crouched, ready to Change and kill the assailant of her mate, but Jax's attacker looked shockingly familiar. He had Jax's face. Same height and build, just different tattoos across his arms, and a single, long scar that zigzagged down his cheekbone.

"Cut it out, fucker," Jax muttered, locking up with him and wrestling. It was funny watching two grown-ass giant men play-fight like little kids.

"Ma!" his twin yelled as Jax got him in a head lock. "Ma! Ma, Ma, Ma, Ma, M—"

"Holy hell nuggets, what, Jathan?" a tiny woman in a yellow polka dot tankini yelled over her shoulder from where she sat in a bright orange chair. She had brightly dyed red hair and wore sixties-style horn-rimmed sunglasses and a floppy straw hat. In her hand was one delicious-looking purple beverage that Annalise was pretty sure was some type of pomegranate flavored beer.

Jathan twisted and escaped the headlock, then shoved off Jax and straightened up. "Your least favorite son has returned."

So, that was Willa. Even wracked with waves of pain, Annalise smiled at the way Willa's face transformed when she laid eyes on her son. She'd never witnessed a bigger smile.

The tiny Second of the Gray Backs screamed and high-kneed it across the sandy beach, her brightly painted red toes digging in with each step until she reached Jax and threw her arms around him.

Jax caught the little wrecking ball and picked her up off the ground with his hug. "Hey, Ma." He probably had fifteen inches of height over her, but she was squeezing his neck so hard his words had come out strangled.

It was so fucking cute seeing her giant, muscled-up, tatted-up, badass mate rest his cheek on top of his mother's head and swing her gently. Up until the point Willa wiggled out of his arms and shoved him in the chest. "Village idiot, you can't pick up your damn phone anymore? I called you three times."

"You called twenty-four times, like a psychopath, and I wasn't ready to talk," Jax said without missing a beat.

Willa narrowed her soft brown eyes, the same color as her son's, and arched her gaze to Annalise. "Are you her?"

Annalise stood there confused, her body humming with the urge to Change. "Am I who?"

"Are you the one who is gonna fix my boy?"

Annalise shook her head, baffled. "He doesn't need fixing."

"Oh, good," Jathan said with a grin. "Jax found a lunatic. A hot lunatic, though." He nodded at Jax with a wink. "Good one, bro."

When Jax shoved him hard in the shoulder, Jathan took two harsh steps backward and flipped him off.

Willa took a step closer, dragging a calculating gaze to Annalise's neck, right where Jax had bitten her, then back to her eyes. The tiny woman felt much bigger than her frame, though. She was heavy, dangerous, and she was standing too damn close to Jax, and therefore too damn close to She-Devil. Annalise snarled and doubled over. Desperate to hold onto her skin, she put her hand out and pleaded, "Don't come any closer. I can't...I can't stop her." A panther scream clawed its way up her throat, and this was it. This was the moment that had mortified her to think about. The moment when she would shame Jax in front of his people and show them how broken she'd become.

All she'd wanted was for them to accept her for him. For them to like her. She wanted to fit in and be like everyone else. Even if it was just for one day, or two days, she'd needed the break from the suck so badly. And now She-Devil would ruin everything.

"You gotta beast in you too, girl," Willa said, squatting in the sand. Her eyes were glowing now, the same bright green as Jax's when he got worked up.

"Willa?" A tall man layered in muscles with long, horrifying scars all over his torso asked. "What's happening?"

"Your son brought home a monstah kitty." But Willa was smiling eerily, and other shifters were starting to gather around them.

Too many bodies. Too many people. Too heavy. The scent of fur and dominance was everywhere, and She-Devil couldn't be contained anymore. She ripped out of Annalise with a roar, and it hurt so bad for that blinding moment of Change.

Time slowed. She wished it hadn't because what she witnessed in the three seconds it took for She-Devil to recover from the Change was horrifying.

Willa shifted first into a towering she-grizzly. Jax and Jathan's bears exploded from them, and behind the trio of monster brown bears, the others, who had been relaxing in chairs, shifted. Bears and boars and gorillas came rushing toward her.

Annalise was too small in this body. She didn't have control. She barely had a loud enough voice to warn She-Devil. *Don't attack or they'll kill you.*

With another scream, She-Devil charged Willa because she was the dangerous one here. Jathan's dark chocolate bear was confused and backing away, and Jax's bear stood there on its hind legs with his eyes locked passively on She-Devil, waiting, but Willa would be a fun fight. She would be a challenge. She would be even more fun to bleed than Barret.

Full of mindless red rage, She-Devil leapt through the air and hit Willa in the chest, but then was promptly tossed into the center of all the monster animals of Damon's Mountains. She'd just been fed to the bears.

Fine. She would just kill them all.

Annalise was panicking at She-Devil's stupid plan. This was like all the other times she stole her body. She made the worst decisions for their survival. Stupid panther.

She connected with a blond grizzly and was swatted back down to earth. Pain slashed across her back end as she took a set of vicious claws there. This wasn't fun. She was losing. Not only losing the Blood Game, but for the first time in her existence, She-Devil realized she had even more to lose. Like her life. There were too many of them, and more were pouring onto the bank from the river. When a pitch-black grizzly charged the circle, She-Devil crouched down on her belly and backed up, almost into Willa, who raked a massive paw right across her backside. It hurt so fucking bad. She-Devil spun and hissed, swatted out a paw, which Willa ducked neatly. The others were closing in, and it would be a dog pile soon. She-Devil flattened her ears and let off a warning growl as the Black grizzly shouldered his way into the circle. His black eyes were full of fury as he barreled down on her. She flattened herself to the ground in terror. His gigantic paws rivaled the size of Jax's, and he slammed them down on either side of her body and roared in her face.

She-Devil rolled over on her back and lay there, stunned. And bleeding. And angry, hurt, and confused. The black grizzly would kill her now. She could see it in his eyes. They'd gone dead. Alpha. Creed. He was so dominant, like Willa, like Jax.

She wasn't in Red Havoc territory anymore. She

was in Hell! This wasn't fun anymore, and she wanted out of here.

A deafening roar sounded from the circle, and she hunched at how pissed-off Jax sounded. Even he was scary right now. All of She-Devil's bravado left her, and then she did something she'd never done before.

She ran.

Not literally, but she shrank and gave Annalise back her skin like a scaredy-cat.

Aching all over, Annalise lay between those giant paws with her arms flung over her face, just waiting on the death blow.

Growling with every breath, the bear eased back, though, and left her there. The other animals backed off, too, all except Jax who paced close to her, eyeing the others.

She didn't know what to do as everyone started shifting back to their human forms and talking low amongst themselves. They'd all been having a good time at the river until she'd come along and ruined it.

"That's a bad kitty," a dark headed behemoth said from where he stood by a grill. Apparently he hadn't felt threatened enough by her to shift with the others. He wore an orange apron that had music notes on it and said *let me see the pizza roll*. "Shifting here like that will get you spankings. How's your butt feel?"

Annalise didn't even want to see the claw marks. They stung so bad, and now they had sand in them. Already she was angled on her side, resting on one hip, trying to give it relief. She'd gotten a public bear spanking? And from the mother of the man she loved. She was blushing from head to toe with mortification. "My butt feels not great," she admitted.

"Cool," he said, his dark eyebrows lifting high. "Are you hungry?"

Mostly she was naked, embarrassed, sore, and she had sand in her crack, but okie dokie, her stomach growled at the scent of cheese and meat and dough that wafted her way. "Yes?" she said in a small voice, more question than anything.

"Bash will get you fixed up with food," a very naked Willa said, holding her hand out to help Annalise up.

Annalise hesitated, not understanding. Willa had just hurt her, and now she was helping her?

Willa huffed a sigh and reached down, grabbed her wrist and yanked her upward with surprising strength. "You're a violent little beasty." She cracked a naughty grin. "I like that about you. Plus, I heard a rumor you took Almost Alpha in the Red Havoc Crew."

"No, just Second."

"Potato, tomato," Willa said, shrugging one shoulder up and searching the ground for something.

That wasn't how the rhyme went, but okay. Jax had Changed back and was cracking a smirk. Bash shoved a paper plate with a dozen pizza rolls into one of her hands and a fruity beer with a miniature pink umbrella into the other, and everything was weird.

"Everyone," Jax called, cupping a hand on one side of his mouth. "This is Annalise of Red Havoc. She's mine."

"Hi, Annalise," the butt-naked shifters said in unison as they went back about their business like they hadn't all just shifted for battle.

As he passed, Jathan clapped Annalise so hard on the back she coughed. Bash tossed him a pizza roll through the air, and Jax's twin caught it in his mouth like a circus poodle. He turned and walked backward a couple steps, grinning at her as he chewed. "I always wanted a sister to torture," he said around the bite. "I mean a sister besides Jax."

A football sailed through the air and hit Jathan smack dab in the forehead, and when she turned around, Jax was smiling remorselessly. Bash belted a laugh that sounded like the bray of a donkey.

None of this should've been funny. None of it. That didn't stop Annalise from laughing disproportionately loudly at their antics and at this surreal and strange moment. These crazy Gray Backs, Boarlanders, and Ashe Crew...they reminded her a little of Red Havoc. Of the boys teasing constantly, reacting in ways she never would've expected. That battle and bear claw spanking had reminded her of the way Barret, Anson, Greyson, and Ben had protected She-Devil for days from those lions, trying their best to keep her in control without really hurting her.

For a tiny instant, she almost felt...homesick.

Shaking her head hard at that idiotic thought, she looked over at Jax, who had a mouthful of something. Her plate now only sported half the food it once did. "You stole my food?"

"I'm so freaking hungry," he said with a full mouth.

When he reached for another, she swatted his

hand and yanked the plate away. "Get your own."

"Mean and greedy," he accused through a grin, but he sauntered off toward Bash's grill.

As she watched him load up a plate, talking and laughing with Bash and Jathan, it struck her how relaxed he was right now. It wasn't like with Red Havoc, when the fur along his back was bristled all the time. Where he was ready to fight and bleed the cats at any given moment.

Here, he wasn't battle ready. He was just Jax.

He was Gray Back, and she was Red Havoc, and if they were going to stay together, one of them was going to have to make a very big sacrifice.

FOURTEEN

It was dark in Jax's trailer except for the soft moonlight that filtered in through the blinds, covering the bedroom in blue stripes. Annalise was lying on her belly on his bed, smiling over at him, because he couldn't seem to stop smiling either. She was naked as a jaybird because she was trying to get her butt to heal faster. Jax had bandaged it and taken care of her, and they'd hung out in here for the rest of the evening and into the night, just the two of them. It had been relaxed, and they'd talked for hours. And She-Devil had stayed silently pouting inside of her, giving her muscles time to relax and heal. Thank goodness for her quick shifter healing, too, because she was feeling like a new woman, and more hopeful than she had in a week.

It had been the perfect night.

"I want to show you something," Jax murmured, stroking her hair from her face.

"I've already seen your dick. Very impressive."

He chuckled low, his white teeth flashing in the dark. "Thank you for saying that."

"I mean it. That thing's like…Thor Dick."

He buried his face in the pillow and cracked up. He sighed and looked over at her again, the corners of his eyes crinkling with his smile. "Tell me the next one."

With a put-upon sigh, Annalise propped herself up on her elbows and read the next on the list. "Number eight, get a motherfuckin' job."

"Where did you work before?"

"Before She-Devil? Because you know I wasn't working while I was my own one-animal circus act."

His smile widened. "Yeah, before the bite. Where did you work?"

"The post office."

He inhaled deeply and feigned shock. "You were a postal worker."

"Yeah, it was super-sexy," she said in her best

phone sex operator voice. "I wore this blue, button-down, short-sleeved shirt and navy pants over my granny panties that made my butt look like two flap-jacks—"

"God, stop." Jax was laughing again. "Did you like your job?"

"I loved it. There were some really nice ladies who worked there with me. And the people who would come in were usually nice and talkative. It was a low-stress job, good benefits. I was happy. Content. What are you doing?" she asked, swatting his glowing phone away from his face. "Pay attention to me. I was telling you important stuff!"

"I'm looking up the post office in Covington. I want to mark more off the list."

Okay, that was actually really sweet. "Anything?"

"It says they're hiring."

"Really?"

"Yeah, look." He showed her the screen. "So there's more motivation to be bigger than She-Devil because your dream post office job could be right there." He bit his lip in that sexy-boy way and let off a low rumble. "I can't fuckin' wait to see your sexy flapjacks in those navy man-pants."

She giggled and said, "Okay, number nine, steal a car to get me to the super-awesome job I find."

"Oh, mark that off. I can take care of that."

"What? No. You aren't buying me a car."

"Wait, why don't you have a car? Everyone has a car, Anna."

"I did have a car until I had an uncontrolled Change in it. Apparently, She-Devil doesn't know how to drive, and it smashed into a tree and was totaled. And then she scratched up the seats and pissed in it. Insurance gave me some money. I just haven't replaced it yet."

"Your animal's the worst," he said through a smile that said he was teasing her.

"But really, she is."

"Nah, she's not so bad."

"She attacks everyone."

"Not me."

Annalise propped her elbow on the pillow and rested her cheek in her hand. Huh. "She *hasn't* ever attacked you. I didn't think about that until now."

"It's because she like-likes me."

"Or she's in heat and she saw Maximus."

"Babe. Did you just name my dick Maximus?"

"It was that or call it a worm again."

Jax dragged her close and tickled her ribs as he rubbed his beard against her neck. With a squeal, she squirmed against him, then peeled into a fit of giggles until he released her.

"You're even better in person," he said suddenly.

The butterflies were back with his spontaneous compliment. "Really?"

"Yeah. I was afraid that if we ever met, you wouldn't be like you were when we texted. You wouldn't be as positive and nice. You wouldn't be as caring. But you're so much better than I imagined."

"That's because you have a crappy imagination."

"Accept my compliments, woman."

"Same."

"What?"

She smiled because she was feeling mushy right now. "I feel the same. About you. You're so much better than I could've ever imagined."

He searched her eyes for a few moments before he murmured, "Go back to number two."

From heart, she recited, "Make him fall in love with me asap."

"Mark it off."

Her entire body warming with a happy blush, she picked up the purple pen and marked off number two.

"Next."

"Call Samuel so he doesn't worry. It's too late to do that one tonight. I could text him. That would be close enough."

"Yeah, do that."

While she was typing an *I'm okay and doing better* text to her brother, Jax read off the next one. "Find a magical serum to cure shifter-dom, aka kill She-Devil." The smile faded instantly from his lips, and his face settled into a troubled expression.

Annalise hit send on Samuel's text and then asked, "What's wrong?"

"I don't like this one. I don't like you talking about killing her. She-Devil is part of you. I like her. I want you to keep her."

"Well, I don't have a choice. There's no cure."

"Yes, there is. Ben didn't always have his panther. I researched him. He was in Apex, some genetic cleansing lab that stripped animals out of shifters. Most of the time it killed them, but sometimes it worked. It worked on Ben. He didn't get his panther back for years after he was in that lab. I don't want you to kill your cat. I want you to own her."

Something about his impassioned speech made She-Devil draw up a little. She wasn't pouting anymore. She was listening. And Annalise felt a surge of pride in herself. Maybe she could do that someday and be the woman Jax deserved. He deserved a strong mate. He had faith in her, wanted her to be a badass, wanted her to be a better shifter, and it was strong motivator right here, right now.

He drew her palm to his lips and pressed a kiss there, then said low, "Don't talk about killing her anymore because if you did that, you wouldn't be you."

"Okay," she whispered.

He looked down at her journal again before she realized what number they were on.

"Twelve," he said, "Marry Jaxon and have a dozen of his..." He paused and grinned before he continued. "Monster bear-panther babies."

"Oh, my gosh, now I'm really embarrassed," she said, burying her face in her pillow. "That was a joke. Don't run away from me."

"Oh, no, I'm not running. I'm gonna put at least

two dozen monster babies in you," he said, punching out his words through his soft laughing. "Okay, number thirteen." He stopped talking, so she looked up at him. He wore a frown again as he read it silently. He inhaled sharply and read. "Thirteen, live happily ever after in the woods with a bunch of gross boys who I'm pretty sure are making moonshine on the mountain behind my cabin." Jax scratched his lip with the back of his thumbnail. "My cabin," he repeated. "Does Red Havoc feel like a den? Like a home?"

"Yes," she said, confused. "That was the point of me moving out there though, right?"

Jax nodded and offered her a sad smile. "You found your place."

"My place is with you."

"A rogue."

"So…I'll be a rogue, too, then."

His frown deepened, and he wouldn't meet her eyes. "I want to show you something."

Ah, there was that subject change he'd been so damn good at in their text messages. She knew from experience there was no turning him back to the subject that had run him off in the first place. With a sigh, she said, "Okay, Jax, show me."

FIFTEEN

Annalise stared up at the tree house high in the branches of a sturdy oak. The wood was worn, old, and gray from its battle against the elements. But some of the planks of the house had been replaced with new wood, and recently if the scent of lingering sawdust was anything to go by.

She squeezed Jaxon's hand and looked up at him. "You're giving me something important, aren't you?"

He dipped his chin once.

"What does it mean to you?"

"When I was a kid, maybe seven or eight, I started having these urges to leave my trailer at night. My parents would be so pissed when I came back and would ask where I'd been all night, but I couldn't tell them. There wasn't an answer. I just...wandered. Eventually they got used to it. Sometimes Jathan would come with me, but he got bored of walking the woods in the dark. As I got older, Titan wanted to wander farther, and the urges got worse. I had to leave during the day, too. Take breaks from work to go...anywhere. Beaston built this treehouse a long time ago. The kids I grew up with, Harper Keller, Air Ryder, Aaron Keller, Wyatt James, Weston Novak, my brother, Bash's kids, Beaston's kids, all the kids who grew up in Damon's Mountains...this was like a hideaway. Countless hours were spent playing here and shifting in these woods, learning how to depend on the other kids around us. Like a miniature crew. The next generation. But for me, those lessons on how to be a crew slid right over me. I would come here more and more when I knew nobody would be here. Late at night, when everyone was asleep in their trailers, I would wander for hours and usually end up here because home didn't feel like home, and I had nowhere else that Titan felt a connection to."

"What are you saying, Jax?"

When he looked back down at her, his eyes were glowing green. "I'm saying, you found a steady home in Red Havoc. *My cabin*, you said. This treehouse is the closest I ever got to *my cabin*, and as we speak, Titan is asking me to leave these woods and roam."

Flap, flap, scritch, scratch.

Annalise jerked her attention to a branch by the tree house. A large raven sat there, one dark eye on her.

Flap, flap. She ruffled her wings, then scraped her shiny black beak against the bark of the branch under her.

Flap, flap. The raven spread her wings and dove straight for Annalise.

She-Devil stayed inside of her skin as she ducked away from the dive-bombing raven at the last moment. The bird arced low to the pine-needle blanketed forest floor and then lifted just enough to land on a man's arm.

Annalise startled badly. She hadn't heard him approach, and there was something quite scary about the way he stared at her. Like he could see right through to her soul with those glowing green eyes, the same color as Jax's. The man's head was canted like a curious animal, and even from way over here, she could feel dominance wafting from him.

Monster, She-Devil warned, but she didn't push for a Change. She was still uncertain after the fight earlier.

The man's hair was chestnut-colored and mussed on top. He wore jeans and a navy sweater that clung to his rigid musculature.

"Beaston," Jax greeted him. "I was wondering where you were. You asked me to bring her to you, but you didn't show up at the river."

"I was there at the river," Beaston said, giving his attention to the large raven on his forearm. He ran a knuckle down its chest. "I wanted to watch her first. Watch the panther. She-Devil."

The way he said her animal's name so intimately drew chills up Annalise's spine.

"I've seen you a long time."

"I-I don't think we've met," Annalise stammered.

"Sure we did. Don't you remember the night you were bitten?"

Pain slashed through her head as something tugged right at the edge of her memory.

No, She-Devil pleaded.

"I was too late," Beaston said, his eyes still on the raven as he petted her. "I'm always too late. I wanted to fix you before you got broken, but fate never lets me win. Jax calls you his Anna. Did you know?" Beaston slightly lifted his arm with the raven on it. "This is my Ana. You two are alike but different. Black feathers. Black fur. She was in a cage once, too." Beaston slid that eerie green gaze to Annalise. "Strong women don't do well in cages. I was there that night, just too late."

Flashes of her fighting Brody as he dragged her into the bedroom blasted across her mind.

Tears welled in Annalise's eyes, and she shook her head. She'd blocked out this memory for so long. She didn't want to see it again, but something inside of her said she must.

Pain. She screamed for help. He bit her hard, and then it wasn't her screaming anymore. It was the panther. And then there was silver fur and long, sharp claws, but they weren't hers. Blood. Brody staring with dead, vacant eyes at the ceiling as she cowered in the corner, watching in terror as the huge silver grizzly bear avenged her.

She hadn't killed Brody after all.

Beaston had.

"You got hurt, but I thought about it. I could see what was going to happen. I dreamed of you. I could see you would be Jax's, and so I'm not angry at me anymore. Fate was right to hurt you. She broke you into the exact right shape to fit Jaxon. Like she did to my Ana. Like she did to me." Beaston swallowed hard, his Adam's apple bobbing as he arced his gaze to Jax. "Your mother will miss you."

"What do you mean," Jax asked, his voice tainted with confusion.

"Always a rogue until you found your Anna."

Jax shook his head and seemed utterly baffled. "I'm still rogue. I want to roam now. Nothing's changed."

"Where were you for the last two weeks?" Beaston asked, lifting his chin and looking smug, as if he knew the answer already.

Beside Annalise, Jax went quiet and still.

"Where?" Beaston demanded, voice crackling with power.

"Red Havoc territory."

A feral smile took Beaston's face for just a moment before it slipped off again. "You are a rogue here but not with the panthers. You picked your Anna. Titan will be with her like glue. She picked your home. You don't belong in Damon's Mountains anymore, Jax." He turned and strode off into the woods. "Follow me, Jax's Anna. I made you a present to say I'm sorry for being too late that night."

Shocked, Annalise looked up at Jax, who was still frozen like a river in an Alaskan winter, eyes stuck to where Beaston was disappearing into the woods.

"Jax?" she asked, slipping her hand into his. "I think Beaston saved me that night."

Jax inhaled sharply and ran his hand down his beard. "Come on," he urged, pulling her after Beaston.

It seemed like they walked for hours, but maybe it was only minutes. Her head was spinning with the memories from that night. She-Devil had helped hide them from her all this time because she'd been so scared. So angry. She wanted to hurt everyone because she'd been hurt.

They followed the man with the deep limp through the dark woods as the raven on his arm watched them with soft brown eyes.

And as they came to a clearing, Jax slowed and stared in awe at the cream colored singlewide mobile home with a red door and forest green shutters. It was hooked to an eighteen-wheeler. The house numbers were shiny and new, but had been nailed on strangely. The last zero was dangling upside down.

1010.

"Holy shit," Jax whispered, his chest heaving. "Beaston, is this what I think it is?"

"I made a replica of the old trailer because I can see how hard it will be for Red Havoc to become what they need to become. They are like the Ashe Crew, like the Gray Backs, like the Boarlanders, but there's no magic up in those mountains. Not yet. I made this with pieces of the original. Light fixtures, the cabinets, the bathroom sinks. Things I saved when ten-ten fell apart." Beaston turned to her. "Jax's Anna." He ducked his chin, and such sincerity pooled in his inhuman eyes when he said, "This is my 'I'm sorry.'"

Annalise didn't understand why he would give her a mobile home. Or how he knew so much. How he'd known to be there that night, or about She-Devil. But inside of her, She-Devil was breaking apart. Her anger was evaporating, and she was in mourning. The armor was gone from her animal, and some bone-deep instinct said it was time to start healing, for both Annalise and for She-Devil.

She didn't understand the gift, but she knew from

the moisture that rimmed Jax's and Beaston's eyes, that it was huge and meaningful.

"You never had anything to say I'm sorry for," she said, warm tears streaming down her cheeks. Her bottom lip trembled, so she bit it and drew in a shaky breath before she stepped forward and hugged Beaston up tight. He went rigid in her arms, but that was okay. "Thank you for being there that night, Beaston. Thank you for protecting me and for not letting me be alone."

Slowly, Beaston lifted his free arm and patted her back gently. And then he eased away and glanced at her, then Jax, then the trailer. Without another word, he gave her a slight smile, which still looked feral as hell, and then turned on his heel and disappeared into the woods with his Ana on his arm.

Jax wrapped his arms around Annalise from behind, and together they stood staring at the trailer, his cheek resting on hers.

"Jax?" she asked at last.

"Yeah?"

"I think maybe I'm ready to go home."

She could feel his smile against her cheek. Jax pressed a kiss right over the claiming mark on her neck and murmured, "Me, too."

SIXTEEN

"No," Anson said, looking grumpy with his arms over his chest. "This ain't a trailer park. It's a nice, respectable—"

"Moonshine distillery?" Annalise dead-panned. "Also, there is a pile of car parts over there that've probably been there for years," she said, pointing. "And all your No Trespassing signs have bullet holes in them. I've been sleeping in a cabin that is missing its entire front half, which is covered with rope and a blue tarp. I woke up to a mouse eating my cereal last week." She scrunched up her face. "Its testicles were huge."

"The trailer is growing on me," Ben said, nodding at 1010, where Jax and Greyson were unhooking it from the eighteen-wheeler.

"Why can't we just fix the damn cabin?" Barret asked.

"Well, we're going to, but until then, Annalise can sleep in the trailer," Ben murmured.

"About that," Jax called. "I'm staying in it, too."

"No," all of the panthers in Red Havoc yelled at once.

"As Almost Alpha, I feel like my vote should count extra," Annalise said with a grin.

Ben narrowed his eyes in annoyance. "It's not Almost Alpha. It's called Second, and for that shit to be official, you have to pledge to my crew."

"Cool. Me and Jax are ready whenever you are. Hey, Jenny!" she called, waving to the alpha's mate who was standing on their porch, leaned on the railing, grinning.

Jenny gave an easy wave. "Hey, Almost Alpha, you back to kick Barret's ass some more?"

"Ha!" Barret blasted out. "Ha, ha, ha. I hate you and you and you," he said, pointing to each of the crew in turn. And then he flipped off the trailer and marched over to a water hose on the side of the nearest cabin, turned it on, and pointed the end at them. Then waited. And waited.

"Dear dumbass," Anson drawled, "that faucet doesn't work."

Barret yelled and threw the dry hose down, then stomped off into the woods. A panther scream sounded a couple of seconds later, and Anson and Greyson snorted in amusement.

Even Ben cracked a smile. "Why do you want to be a part of my crew, Grizzly. This is panthers only."

"Well, my mate is a panther, and she picked this place, so I'm settling. You can let me in, or I'm just going to hang out here, pestering the shit out of you until you do. I'm unpledged, been a rogue since I was eighteen, and I have a big stake in this crew."

"Being?" Jenny asked from where she was approaching, holding little Raif's hand.

"Being this pretty kitty right here," he said, making his way toward Annalise. He wore faded blue jeans, and his tight, white T-shirt was streaked with dirt from unloading 1010, but under his baseball cap, his smile was bright and easy, like it had been in Damon's Mountains. He draped his arm over her shoulders, and she instinctively leaned in closer to be nearer to him, and to feel the warmth and safety he always blanketed her with. She-Devil purred.

"Wherever she goes, I go," Jax said. "She wants to be Second of Red Havoc, so here I am. You'll have the fealty of my bear when things go south here, Ben. And they will. You know it and I know it. I'll back you in whatever decisions you make for the crew so long as they keep Annalise safe."

Ben shook his head and kicked at the dirt with the toe of his boot. At least he hadn't given a hard no yet. Sensing weakness, Annalise pounced. "Think about it. You and the boys won't have to watch me at night anymore. Jax is a grizzly and protective of me. He can handle any of my night shifts on his own. You can sleep."

"I think you'll be good for the crew, Annalise. I vote yes for both of them," Greyson said, raising his hand and shocking the ever-lovin' shit out of her. That was way more than a single syllable caveman grunt. She was going to mark off number five on her short-term-goals list as soon as she had her journal in hand again.

"I vote yes," Jenny said quietly.

"I like bears," Raif said earnestly, raising his hand like he was in school.

Ben looked at Anson, who rolled his eyes and raised two relaxed fingers. "I like fighting."

Ben gritted his teeth so hard a muscle twitched in his jaw. "Before I consider letting a goddamn dominant Gray Back grizzly into my crew, Annalise, you have to tell me something."

"Okay, shoot."

"Tell me what this crew means to you."

Annalise smiled. "It means home. I know what you all were doing out in those woods—protecting me from myself, protecting me from the lions. I watched you exhaust yourself. Ben, I started thinking you were going to put me down, but you gave Jax a chance to help me instead. You're a good alpha. I want to be a better panther, be a better shifter, and I know you can help me. And maybe someday I can be valuable to this crew, too. I don't feel so sick anymore. So unsteady. I think I can do this, be a good Second if I work hard enough. I want that. It gives me something to aim for. But I can't join your crew without Jax." She wrapped her arms around his waist and rested her head against his pec. "I picked him before I ever met him. Grizzly, human, panther, it wouldn't matter to me. He's just my Jax, and I'm his

Anna."

Ben shook his head. "I can't fuckin' believe I'm about to do this."

"Do it," Jenny drawled.

"Dooo iiiit," Anson said. "I love stupid-decision Sundays."

Ben cleared his throat and crossed his arms over his chest, lifted his chin high, and smiled down at Annalise. "I thought I was going to lose another one, and it ripped me up. I couldn't sleep. Couldn't eat. I was sick, just thinking about you not being salvageable. Whatever Jax did to help you...I owe him." Deep emotion welled in the alpha's eyes, and he cleared his throat hard. "Jax and Annalise, welcome to Red Havoc." He turned and wrapped his arm around Jenny's shoulders and kissed her on the side of the head as he walked them back to their cabin.

"We're still not the C-team though, so fuck you," Anson said, shoving a middle finger in Jax's face.

Jax snapped his teeth and barely missed biting his finger off.

Anson yelped and slunk toward his cabin. "I'm not scared of you," he said when he was almost there, but he did check over his shoulder a couple of times.

Greyson gave them a half smile, then made his way back to 1010, climbed up in the big rig, and drove it away from the trailer. In the woods, Barret's panther screamed again.

"Are you sure this is the life you want?" Jax asked, hands on her hips as he turned her slowly to face him.

Annalise scanned the clearing, from the row of cabins, to 1010 sitting in the evening shadows of the Appalachian Mountains, back to the man she loved. Inside of her, She-Devil was quiet and steady, watching her mate. Everything she wanted was right here. "I think it's the life I need. I think maybe Beaston was right. I used to think the bite was a curse, but now I think fate was giving me a gift instead. I had to go through what I went through so I could appreciate you. So I could be stronger. I used to wish for my old life," she said, slipping her hands up his chest and around his neck. "I just wanted to be steady again, but there was no adventure back then. Every day was the same. Maybe I was stunted by normalcy. Now I think I wouldn't really understand joy if I hadn't learned how bad things can get. And I know I would've never understood how much I could shoulder if I hadn't been tested. Jax," she murmured through an emotional smile, "we'll never be alone again."

Jax looked so damn proud. "I wouldn't change a single thing about you, Anna."

But she knew what he really meant. Lifting to her tiptoes, she pressed her lips to his and hugged him tightly. And when she eased away, she whispered, "I love you, too."

Today was the first day of the rest of her life when she would get to mark one of the last numbers off her list. She would live happily ever after in the woods with a bunch of gross boys who were probably making moonshine on the mountain behind the cabins.

This moment right here, standing in front of 1010, nestled in the mountains that called to her heart, safe and warm and whole in the arms of the man she adored, she, Annalise, Almost Alpha of the Red Havoc Crew, had found the life she wanted.

T. S. JOYCE

Want more of these characters?

Red Havoc Rogue is the first book in the Red Havoc Panthers.

For more of these characters, check out these other books from T. S. Joyce.

Red Havoc Rebel
(Red Havoc Panthers, Book 2)

Red Havoc Bad Cat
(Red Havoc Panthers, Book 3)

This is a spinoff series set in the Damon's Mountains universe. Start with Lumberjack Werebear to enjoy the very beginning of this adventure.

About the Author

T.S. Joyce is devoted to bringing hot shifter romances to readers. Hungry alpha males are her calling card, and the wilder the men, the more she'll make them pour their hearts out. She werebear swears there'll be no swooning heroines in her books. It takes tough-as-nails women to handle her shifters.

She lives in a tiny town, outside of a tiny city, and devotes her life to writing big stories. Foodie, wolf whisperer, ninja, thief of tiny bottles of awesome smelling hotel shampoo, nap connoisseur, movie fanatic, and zombie slayer, and most of this bio is true.

Bear Shifters? Check

Smoldering Alpha Hotness? Double Check

Sexy Scenes? Fasten up your girdles, ladies and gents, it's gonna to be a wild ride.

For more information on T. S. Joyce's work,
visit her website at
www.tsjoyce.com